Praise for *Strawgirl*

'Kay's language has a vigour a̶n̶ [...] by surprise with its aptness and [...] touches add a sparkle to the book'
Adèle Geras, *Guardian*

'A lyrical story that leaves much to the imagination as well as being a quick-moving adventure'
Guardian

'An immediately involving and intriguing story skilfully told with a touch of magic realism. It embraces important themes: loss, loyalty, bereavement, bullying and identity'
Times Educational Supplement

'A stunningly gifted new children's author is the poet Jackie Kay, whose *Strawgirl* is a blend of lyric and adventure'
Amanda Craig, *Independent on Sunday*

'Kay has written a warm and comforting story in which elements of traditional folk myths are yoked to a world recognizable to today's children . . . an out-of-the-ordinary tale of enchantment'
Carole Mansur, *Daily Telegraph*

'Kay distracts from the sadness of Maybe's situation with moments of lovely poetic feyness'
The Scotsman

'A flowing, lyrical story about self-confidence and awareness, it ploughs a furrow through solitude and isolation, bigotry and bullying. Highly recommended'
Manchester Evening News

'*Strawgirl* is a rewarding read for anybody who enjoys lovely writing and gentle humour'
Glasgow Sunday Herald

Jackie Kay was born in Edinburgh in 1961 and grew up in Glasgow. She has won the Signal Award twice for her children's poetry collections, *Two's Company* and *The Frog Who Dreamed She Was an Opera Singer*. She has also published three adult poetry collections, the first of which, *The Adoption Papers*, won the Saltire and Forward Prizes. The second, *Other Lovers*, won a Somerset Maugham Award. *Trumpet* (Picador), her first novel, won the Author's Club First Novel Award and the Guardian Fiction Prize. *Why Don't You Stop Talking* (also Picador), a collection of short stories, was published recently. *Strawgirl* is her first novel for children.

JACKIE KAY

Strawgirl

MACMILLAN CHILDREN'S BOOKS

First published 2002 by Macmillan Children's Books

This edition published 2003 by Macmillan Children's Books
a division of Macmillan Publishers Limited
20 New Wharf Road, London N1 9RR
Basingstoke and Oxford
www.panmacmillan.com

Associated companies throughout the world

ISBN 0 330 48063 4

1 3 5 7 9 8 6 4 2

A CIP catalogue record for this book is available
from the British Library.

Phototypeset by Intype London Ltd
Printed and bound in Great Britain by
Mackays of Chatham plc, Chatham, Kent

For Matthew Kay and Ella Duffy, with love

With many thanks to Alyson Pryde for her expert advice on farming and to my editor, Sarah Davies

1

The Day of the Letter

If you want to get to Wishing Well Farm, drive along the A6Z6 until you come to the B1Q7. Follow the B1Q7 until it joins the unnamed road. Take the left fork, not the right – definitely not the right. Go down this road for 400 metres until you come to a muddy track on your left. Follow this track round to the farm. The stone farmhouse can be glimpsed through the hedges. A rather old sign, **WELCOME TO WISHING WELL FARM,** is visible. It is made of wood and there is a painting of a black-and-white cow next to it, a pint of milk next to the cow. Follow the mud track all the way round to the left, then to the right. The farmhouse can be seen again now and the dairy parlour. There is one last, very large hole in the mud road before you come to the house. Easy does it.

Stop for a minute to look at the old wishing well just before you get to the house. Moss gathers round the old brick walls. It is not a working well any more, but children still make wishes. They throw a penny down into the deep darkness and wish for something crucial. They lean over and try to see where their wish has fallen. They never hear the penny drop. Their faces wear a certain look – tight-closed eyes, furrowed foreheads. You could almost guess what they are wishing for with such devotion, such dedication – a best friend, a new bike, a full apology, a dark, devoted dog.

The farm has been there for hundreds of years and passed on through generations. The MacPhersons run it these days. The farmhouse was built at the turn of the twentieth century. It is slightly dilapidated now, in need of a lick of paint, a new frame for a window. At the front of the farmhouse is an outhouse with a sloping roof. Inside are ten pairs of olive-green wellington boots. They are caked in cow dung and look as if they might walk on their own, when everybody is asleep at night – down the old farm road, from barn to barn to house, wellies on the move.

Round the side of the farmhouse is the first old barn. Wind blows the door open, then shut. The hay swirls and whirls around the barn. For a minute it seems as if something is moving.

A gaggle of geese guards the farm more effectively than pit bulls or Rottweilers or snarling German shepherds. The postman arrives in his red van with a letter. He delivers all letters, ignorant of the sorrow or the joy they will bring, not knowing whether one letter contains news of a death or another a piece of good fortune. He is blissfully unaware that the letter he has just delivered into the open mouth of the letterbox will change everybody's lives. He jumps back in his van and fast-tails it out of there. The postman isn't fond of geese. Their beaks frighten him and their eyes are too intense. The geese chase his van, honking and flapping their powerful wings. The dust from the dirt-track road flies up as the postman drives away.

A brown hen walks into the farmhouse and drops a piece of straw on to the floor. It is a sign that a stranger will be coming to stay.

It is Harvest Time on Wishing Well Farm. Out in the fields on a hot, thirsty day, Maybe MacPherson, her father, Jamie, and Fred, the farmhand, are working hard. Gigantic round bales of straw are shifted by a big tractor with huge horns. Two massive spikes catch the bales and lift them up. They follow the tractor up and down the field. The hay will feed the cows and the straw will keep them warm.

Maybe is a nickname; she is so-called because she never answers 'Yes' or even 'No' to anything. She is addicted to saying 'Maybe', drawn to the lilac world of mights and possibilities, of indecisions and what-ifs. To every direct question, Maybe replies, 'Maybe'. Would you like to go? Would you like to eat? Maybe, maybe, maybe. She drives her family crazy. Her real name is Molly Siobhan MacPherson but no one in her family ever calls her Molly. She is eleven and a bit years old.

She is running alongside the tractor, shouting.

Maybe could tell anyone how a bale of straw is made. The combine cuts the corn stalks low down, nearish to the ground, leaving stubble. It separates grain from straw inside its innards. Straw comes out at the back and lies in lines waiting for the baler. The separated corn comes out of a chute. A tractor and trailer travels alongside the combine and the corn pours into the trailer. Jamie is driving the tractor. He can't hear a word above the din of the machine, so he shouts at Maybe, 'Are you helping or not?'

At the end of the day, Maybe and her father drive the bales of straw into the sheds, where they pile them up at the far end. They are in the middle of preparing the barn for the annual barn dance. They must be the only farmers in the whole of Scotland to still hold a barn dance. It is a good laugh when the harvest is in. They are trying to get the barn spruced up as much as you *can* spruce up a barn. It is not a nice job, let's say. The cows have spent the whole winter in the barn, and there is a pile of cow dung, the size of a baby Ben Nevis to be cleared first.

The MacPs are sweating and hot. They sit down for a break and have some home-made lemonade, made from freshly squeezed lemons, and a slice of Victoria sponge. They chink glasses.

'To the barn dance!' Jamie says.

'To the barn dance,' Maybe replies.

Maybe's father starts to play his African drum and

to sing a Nigerian folk song, 'The Tortoise Sings to the Lion's Farmworkers'. 'Sing after me,' he says.

> '*Leave your hoes and dance with me*. Titi chom
> *Leave your hoes and dance with me*. Titi chom
> *You have come to do the lion's work*. Titi chom
> *Now it's time to enjoy yourselves*. Titi chom.'

Maybe collapses, giggling. 'Don't joke. I canny sing that. '*Titi chom!* What's that when it's at home?'

As they climb up to the top of the stack of bales, Jamie tells Maybe about Nigerian folksongs – how there are spiritual songs, working songs, songs for wayward girls, lullabies. 'Listen to this one!' Jamie says, getting carried away with himself. 'This is a spiritual one.' Jamie sings in his high folky voice:

> '*Do you know the unknown man*
> *Who can change grain into meat?*
> *Do you know the grey old man*
> *Who can change wine into blood?*'

'Wine into blood?' Maybe says. She looks at him as if he is bonkers. She doesn't like it when her father starts to go on about Africa. It makes her feel funny. But Jamie doesn't like the look on her face.

'Don't forget you're an Ibo. Never forget that,' he says, wagging his finger.

'Yeah, yeah,' Maybe says. Sometimes she wishes her dad would get a life. Nobody where they come from in the north-west of Scotland knows what an Ibo is. Or so it seems to Maybe. If she just forgets it, she can get by. Be like the rest of them. Fit in. Her father looks as if she has rejected him. 'How about this for a song?' she shouts from her bale of straw.

> *'Gin a body meet a body*
> *Coming through the rye;*
> *Gin a body kiss a body,*
> *Need a body cry.'*

She walks down one step after another, a staircase made of straw. One hand is at her waist, the other hand in the air:

> *'Coming through the rye, poor body,*
> *Coming through the rye.'*

Jamie laughs. 'Bravo!' he says, 'but you still need to learn that Ibo song. One day you'll have your own children to teach it to. One day I won't be around any more.'

There's a strange rumble of thunder outside. The bales topple over and fall down. 'What's happening, Dad?' Maybe shouts, alarmed. They try to push the bales of straw back on top of each other, but they are too heavy.

'It is a sign from the Ibo gods,' Jamie says, laughing. 'It's as if the bales have minds of their own.'

> 'Gba, gba, gba *on the hollow tree*
> Gba, gba, gba, *who is knocking?'*

'I hope you're joking,' Maybe says, uncomfortable, looking around the barn as if there is somebody else there, some other eerie presence. A cold shiver runs right the way down her spine. 'Brrrr . . .' she says. 'Anybody would think it was winter.'

It is perhaps the first time in Maybe's life that she feels conscious of having a presentiment, a sense of foreboding, a chilly, unspecific knowledge of the future.

Jamie looks at her. 'What's the matter? It's just a few bales of straw toppling. You look like you've seen a ghost.'

'It didn't look like there was going to be thunder,' Maybe says.

'Well, that's the Scottish weather for you. Come on, what's eating you?' Jamie asks.

'Nothing,' Maybe says, but the twist in her stomach is still there, a sinking, sick feeling. 'Tell me about when you came to Scotland,' she says to her dad, and she settles down on the straw bales to listen.

2

The Fight Begins

'When I first came to Scotland, I'd never seen bales before,' Jamie told Maybe.

'Tell me again, why did you come here?' Maybe asked.

'Ah, so you do want to hear a story.'

'Maybe.'

'I've told you it before, you know.'

'I know. But I like this one.'

'You do?' Jamie's eyes gleamed like onyx, like jet, like the eyes of a dark otter that had just spotted a shining silver fish.

'Get on with it,' Maybe said, laughing. She did not like to hand compliments out as if they were sweeties. That was why she was called Maybe. It would take something really quite enormous to get a positive YES out of her. She enjoyed holding this little bit of pleasure back. It meant her parents were always trying to please her rather than her trying to please them, which was, as far as she was concerned, perfectly right. Parents should seek their offspring's approval. Why not? More and more parents these days were trying to impress their children in ways that fooled no kids, certainly not Maybe. They wanted to join in; they wanted their childhood back.

'Thomas and Isabel MacPherson couldn't have children of their own,' Jamie went on. 'A farmer's total nightmare. Nobody to pass their hard work on to. No grandchildren to run about the fields. No grandson to milk the cows. Thomas thought it was something wrong with Isabel, and Isabel thought it was something wrong with Thomas. They tried . . .'

'Tried what?' Maybe asked, a big, dark gleam in her eye.

'You know!' Her dad replied.

'Know what?' Maybe said, smiling again.

'Intercourse, of course,' Jamie said, embarrassed, and Maybe's mouth dropped open.

'*Aiiii!* You said it!' Maybe shrieked.

'They tried and didn't have any luck, so they thought of adopting. They were just about to start the lengthy and frustrating business of becoming pro-spective adoptive parents when a friend came over from Nigeria with me. I was your age. I was eleven,' Jamie said.

'Where were your mum and dad? Why did they abandon you?'

'They were back in Nigeria. They had a dream of having me educated in Great Britain.'

'But you must have missed them!'

'Oh, I did. I did. But Thomas and Isabel were

lovely and they poured all this love that had been waiting for a child straight down my throat. Milky, creamy love.'

'Dad. You've got such a way with that tongue of yours,' Maybe said in her strong, lilting Highland accent. 'Such a tricky wee way, so you have, so you have.'

'So when they died, first Thomas, then Isabel, they left a will that said Wishing Well Farm should be run by me. And lo and behold, at the tender age of twenty-three, I was a tenant farmer and had my own farm. Not long after that, I met your mother and then I had my very own wife. And not long after that, we had you and then I had my very own daughter.' This was the bit of the story that Maybe liked best. He had been telling it to her like this for ever. Even as a wee lassie, she loved hearing it. His tuneful voice saying those words: *my very own daughter.* Oh, it was enough to make even the indecisive sigh with pleasure.

Maybe's mother, Irene MacPherson, an attractive-looking woman with flame-red hair, came into the barn with a worried look on her face. She handed Jamie a letter.

'What's up, Mum?' Maybe asked, curious. Irene was not a worrier. She was usually laid-back, relaxed, easygoing. It was unusual to see her look like this. It gave Maybe a worried feeling herself, right inside her own stomach. 'Mum, what is it?' she said when her mother didn't reply.

'Read this!' Irene said, holding out a letter. 'Would you believe it?'

The letter was from the owners of Wishing Well Farm – two brothers, Mr Harold and Mr Arnold Barnes-Gutteridge, who had purchased the land cheap from the estate of the old laird landowner. The old laird's nephew lived abroad and apparently didn't want the responsibility of owning land.

The letter read:

Dear Mr and Mrs MacPherson,
As you know, your tenancy agreement with the previous owner of this land has now passed on to us, the current owners of the land on which Wishing Well Farm stands. We have formed our own Property Development Agency and are selling off many of our properties to new business ventures. Domino Supermarkets have offered a substantial sum of money to build a large supermarket on the existing land, which would benefit the local community. We are willing to have you rehoused and to offer you some compensation, but in three months the farm will need to be demolished and the cows slaughtered or sold. All previous correspondence from you on this matter, hostile in the extreme, has been passed on to our solicitors.
Yours truly,
Harold and Arnold Barnes-Gutteridge

'What do they mean, demolished?' Maybe asked, appalled and slightly thrilled at the badness of the news, even though she knew the meaning of the word.

'Knocked down,' Jamie said, heavily.

'Blootered.' Irene said.

'Oh!' Maybe said, flattened. 'But it's our farm, it's not their farm.'

'Well, we don't actually own this farm, Maybe, we've explained that before. We rent it from those bloody brothers.'

'Yes, but we run it, we live here, we milk the cows, we plough the land. It's ours.'

'We think so,' Irene said, flapping the letter in her hand. 'Pity the Property Development Agency doesn't see things the same way.'

'We'll fight, won't we, Dad? We won't let it happen.'

'We have been fighting,' her father said between gritted teeth. 'This has been going on for several weeks now, but it's the first time they've mentioned demolishing the farm. Or that we only have three months.'

'You never told me!' Maybe said indignantly.

'You're a child. We can't tell you everything,' Irene said to Maybe.

'Notice they've got the cheek to offer us compensation this time. How can you compensate for a whole way of life?' Jamie said to Irene. 'I'll tell you one thing though,' he went on, 'they'll take this farm over my dead body.'

Four brown hens clucked into the hay shed and settled on a warm bale, peck, pecking away.

3

Cows' Udders

It was time for the afternoon milking. Maybe and Jamie got changed into their red boiler suits and big green wellies. They put on caps to protect their hair. Maybe followed her father through to herd the cows into the dairy. Her wellies trod through cow dung; she called it keech. Some friends from school would get upset if their foot got stuck in a cow keech, but not Maybe. She would tell them it was good for their shoes and that breathing in the rancid, putrid air of a fine cow pat was exceptionally good for the lungs. 'Ahhhhh, breathe deep, girls,' she'd say.

'Gross!' they'd squeal.

The MacPs separated the Dry Cows from the Wet Cows. The Dry Cows were on their two-month sabbatical from being milked. A cow vacation, so it was. It gave the tired old udders a break. The Wet Cows were milked by a milking machine. It could do eight cows at one go. Jamie hooked the cow to the machine; the milk travelled along a pipe and into a jar. When all of the cow's milk was drained out of the udder, the milking machine automatically stopped. The cows were milked twice a day: very early in the morning and around five in the evening. Some cows moved about from foot to foot, restless while they were being milked. Most cows didn't mind the machine; they seemed to enjoy the whole process, as if it were a blessed relief, the milk rushing into the jar, the heavy udder becoming lighter, pinker.

Every cow except Scunnert was milked by machine. Scunnert was frightened of the machine and rebelled. Maybe usually milked Scunnert by hand, pulling each teat quite roughly up and down until the milk was released. Still, one stubborn cow out of sixty-four wasn't bad going. Every cow had a name and a nametag as well as a number for the machine, and each cow knew the time of day when she would be milked and would be waiting at the gate. Each cow progressed, in a stately way, heavy udders swinging, to her appointed stall; everyone knew her own place, where some tasty silage awaited her.

Eight of the cows were Maybe's. These were the special cows that her father had told her were hers from the minute they were born. She had chosen their names herself: Lipstick, Birthday, Bonbon, Violet, Little Pink, Blossom, Pirate and Milkshake. Lipstick, because Maybe's mum had bought a new lipstick when Lipstick was born. Birthday, because she was born on Maybe's birthday, the fourteenth of August. Bonbon, because Maybe had been chewing a bonbon when she was born. Violet, because Maybe's friend

Violet had been round for tea the day she was born. Little Pink, because Little Pink was the smallest one born that morning when the sun was just rising in the sky. Blossom, born when the cherry tree had just blossomed. Pirate, because she had a black patch over her eye. And last, but not least, Milkshake, because she had come straight out and sucked like a maniac, shaking her mother's teats back and forth in the windy night.

Maybe was impatient for the milking to be over. Part of her hated living on a farm, always having so much to do. Her school friends seemed to do very little to help at home. They had very cushy lives. They went home and watched television and ate Doritos. Maybe wasn't allowed to eat any rubbish. Nothing with E-numbers, artificial colours or flavours. Maybe was given things like a raw carrot for her snack, or some fresh salad leaves straight from the garden. Her biggest treats were her mum's home-made cakes: carrot cake, chocolate cake, Victoria sponge, cheese-cake, lemon meringue pie, pineapple upside-down cake – all made with organic flour and eggs and brown raw cane sugar.

Maybe declared herself finished after dipping Scunnert's teats in soothing and disinfecting iodine and glycerine. 'There's more milk in that udder yet,' Jamie said predictably. 'How many times do I have to tell you, get—'

'As much milk as possible,' Maybe said, finishing her father's sentence for him, imitating his voice.

'Well, if you did it, I wouldn't need to say it.'

'Yeah, yeah, yeah, calm down, Dad,' Maybe said.

Jamie frowned, a big, dark crease wrinkling his forehead. 'You're old enough to be more responsible.'

But Maybe wasn't interested in getting as much milk as possible. Not now, not yet. She wanted to watch television so that she could discuss programmes with her friends on Monday. She wanted to watch wrestling because at school everyone was always talking about characters she'd never heard of with great names like The Rock and Stone Cold Steve Austin. She wanted to say on a Monday, 'Wasn't that bad when . . . That was so cool. That was so snide.'

She stared at Scunnert's big udders, at the dirt on the teats, at the cow dung stuck to her behind, at her constantly switching tail. It was a cow's life – not a dog's life, but a cow's life, all right, all right.

4

The Tongs

Maybe tied her maroon-and-blue school tie and buttoned her blazer. She brushed her hair quickly and grabbed her school bag. She had to run to the main road where the school bus picked her up every morning. She waited at the side of the road, looking along it into the distance as if that would make the bus come quicker. The hedge at the side of the road quivered and a magpie flew out, its wings rippling like the notes of a piano, white and black. There was just one magpie, which meant bad luck – a bringer of anger. Maybe knew off by heart the old Scots saying about magpies:

> One means anger, two brings mirth.
> Three a wedding, four a birth.
> Five is heaven, six is hell.
> But seven's the very Devil's ain sell.

She looked around to see if she could see any more magpies. None about, so she spat, a huge glob of spit, sucked backwards into her mouth and then propelled forwards on to the grey country road. That would cancel the bad luck, she hoped, although it was unfortunate that she had seen the lone magpie when she'd just set off on her journey. There were so many omens associated with the magpie and Maybe knew them all. The magpie was the only bird which, according to tradition, refused to enter Noah's Ark.

The sky was light and streaky, like the fat of bacon. There was very little blue up there. The bus appeared in the distance. It trundled to a stop and Maybe climbed on. It was 8:20 a.m.

When Maybe first went to school, she couldn't believe that everybody didn't live on a farm. At Kirsty's house once for tea, she was shocked at the smallness of her garden. Maybe's farm was 400 acres. There was a pine forest in its deep heart where the trees breathed in and out, completely aware of each other's presence, like a single organism. There were crops of barley, wheat and oats. Her mother grew lettuce, cabbage, kale, marrow, onions, turnips, runner beans, potatoes and sugar-snap peas. Irene delighted in her herbs – thyme, basil, mint, tarragon, coriander and rosemary. She had a flower garden as well and loved the Latin names for plants. 'If I had my life again,' she was often saying, 'I would be a horticulturist.'

'A hoity-toity horticulturist,' Jamie would say.

Ms Rose, Maybe's teacher, was doing a lesson on family trees. Most of the class didn't know beyond their grandparents' names. Some didn't even know their full names: they just knew them as Grandma Black or Grandpa Anderson. She seized on Maybe with some enthusiasm. 'Molly, tell us about your family tree,' she said.

'My mum is from Lochinvar and her mother was from Galway and her mother's mother was from Galway too. My mum says she feels just as Irish as she does Scottish,' Maybe said proudly.

'And your father?' Ms Rose asked.

'My father's from Africa.'

'Yes, where exactly? Africa's a continent, not a country.'

'Nigeria,' Maybe muttered. She didn't like it when everybody had to be reminded that she was different.

'Nigeria!' Ms Rose repeated triumphantly. 'And Nigeria is where, exactly? Does anybody know?' Nobody knew, of course.

'On the west coast of Africa,' Maybe muttered.

'Does he have a tribe that he belonged to?' Ms Rose asked.

Maybe wondered if the teacher was genuinely interested or if she was deliberately trying to embarrass her. 'Ibo,' she murmured. 'But he left Nigeria when he was a boy. He's more Scottish now, really.'

'There you are, class – Ibo. Now does anyone know the name of any other African tribes?' Nobody did. They all found the idea very amusing. Maybe prayed she wouldn't have to say Yoruba, Hausa, Ashanti. Her dad had taught her all about the differences between tribes – how the Hausa people were tall and straight, the Ibo small and honest, and the Yoruba unreliable and disloyal. But she kept quiet.

Sharon Harvey had a giggling fit and the tears started to pour helplessly down her face. It was the word 'Ibo'. Ibo! It sounded like *eeee*bo. Her stomach hurt, and the more she tried to stop herself laughing, the more she laughed. Sharon Harvey was sent out of the classroom to calm down in the corridor. Ms Rose had found that shame soon put paid to hysteria. She raised her voice. Aileen Spence was sparked off by Sharon Harvey. Maybe was hurt. She wished they would stop. She felt as if they were laughing at her. Family trees ought to be destroyed. She didn't like harking back, anyway. Why couldn't they all move forward?

Much as Maybe loved her father, she wished that he were just like everybody else so that she could be the same as everybody else too. A little part of her was ashamed of feeling like this. If she were braver, bolder, she'd be proud to be different. At home, she never thought about how she looked, but at school she'd find herself longing to have Sharon Harvey's bunches – to be able to do her hair with pink bobbles. Her hair always grew outwards, like a massive curly halo surrounding her, not down her back the way other girls' hair grew. No, her hair, long, was a massive Afro. Her nose was wider than any girl's in the class. Her lips were thicker. At school, Maybe felt very unusual: the coward inside her wanted to be ordinary, to blend into the background.

'Here in the Highlands, the clans differentiate themselves by wearing different tartans. Who knows about tartans?' Ms Rose asked.

Maybe sighed with relief as a hand shot up and Kirsty Skinner said: 'MacLeod, MacDonald, McIntosh, MacKay, MacCrimmon, Stewart, Fraser, Colquhoun . . .'

'How do the tribes in Nigeria differentiate themselves, Molly?' Ms Rose asked.

Maybe couldn't believe it. She was hot with embarrassment. 'I don't have a clue, Miss,' she said.

'Well, find out for your homework. I want everybody to go home and interview their parents and find out about their family trees. Ask your parents to tell you as much as they know – listen and write it down!' Ms Rose said in her big, booming, important voice, her long fingers banging on her desk. She was fired up even if her students were not. 'History matters. Let's start with our own. Investigate your own bloodlines, see how far back you can go. I promise you'll be absolutely fascinated.'

A few people groaned; nobody looked too excited.

Troy Cameron put up his hand. 'Miss. In Africa they don't wear anything, do they? Or Miss, do they wear grass skirts?' Maybe's cheeks burned. Everybody laughed.

'You're not forgetting, are you, Troy, that your father's father would have worn a Cameron tartan kilt with a great hairy sporran hanging below his knees and plenty of Celtic jewellery? You're not forgetting that he would have had nothing on underneath his kilt, are you, Troy?'

The class laughed even more raucously. Troy flashed Maybe a menacing look, as if she were responsible. The look was enough for her. Somehow Troy Cameron would exact his revenge. She knew it wouldn't be right away: he liked to wait a little. To tease her with the terror of anticipation, with not knowing when exactly he would pounce. This would be a bad one. He had been humiliated and he didn't like it. A thunderous scowl rumbled across his puffy face. A mean fury seemed to swell his cheeks.

At the gate, Troy and his pals, Spider and Moron, were waiting. Moron was so thick he thought his nickname was a compliment. Spider was Spider because of his long spindly limbs and his scratchy voice. Troy didn't need to change his name. He was the leader. Respect. They waited now for Molly Mac-Pherson. The Tongs always called their small encounters with Molly 'teaching her a lesson', as if they were educational. But Maybe was watching out for them today. Last time they had pinned her down and shoved mud into her mouth. But not today. No way. She was ready to run. She was faster than Troy who was a bit of a big fat bloke, faster than Moron who could barely coordinate himself. But Spider was fast. Maybe had a terrifying job beating him.

Spider was right behind her now. She sped down the hill her school was on, down past her bus stop. When she came to the bottom of the hill, she turned right along Balmuildy Road. She ran and ran, out of breath, in the direction of home. She was still far from her farm, at least seven miles. Her heart was beating so loud and fast it hurt. It felt like there was a real live bird trapped inside her, furiously flapping its bright blue wings. Her throat hurt too. She could barely catch her breath. She wanted to collapse, to give in. Something made her continue, something forced her to keep going, on and on and on. Her heart could have actually exploded.

There was the sound of her feet on the road. Then there was the sound of Spider's shoes following. For a moment she was a fox being chased by a hound, a rabbit being pursued by a dog, a deer being hounded by a lion. He was the predator; she was the prey. She risked turning round for a split second, only to see Spider had given up the chase and was standing, folded over himself, his arms hanging down, his body bent at the waist. Troy punched the air a way back in the distance. 'Just you wait, Ibo!' he shouted. 'We're not done with you yet.'

Moron and Troy chanted, 'I-bo! I-bo! I-bo!'

Maybe was still running. She kept on pounding one foot after the other, although she had no need. Fear had made the adrenaline rush and she just could not stop. Even though the Tongs were now way back in the distance, she could still hear the chanting in her head as if she were saying it herself. She tried to shut it out, but it continued getting louder and louder the faster she ran: *Ibo! Ibo! Ibo!* Why did her father have to be an Ibo?

The Tongs made her miss her bus home. It was a walk of several miles along the country roads. She stopped to phone her mum from the red telephone box, but she had no money on her so she had to call the operator and reverse the charges. Her mum hated it when she did that, but of course could never say no in case there was a real emergency.

Maybe heard her mum's resigned voice in the distance say, 'I accept the call.'

'Mum, I've missed my bus,' Maybe whispered, out of breath.

'How did you manage that, Maybe? For goodness sake, you know we're going out tonight! Is this sabotage?'

Maybe didn't have a clue what her mother was talking about. Sometimes her mum was completely bonkers. Sabotage! It was all Maybe needed at the end of her day, a word like that.

'Wait there. I'll come and get you.' Her mother sighed in irritation. 'You're in big trouble for this, young lady. You're grounded.'

Maybe stood waiting for her mother at the side of the road, keeping an eye out for the Tongs. She was shaking and cold. It felt like the worst day of her life. She didn't know it, but the worst was yet to come. Things were only just hotting up. Salty tears poured down her face in fury and self-pity. Nobody knew. Nobody. She never told her parents about the Tongs. It would make them unhappy and her father would probably turn up at the school and embarrass her.

Rain splattered from the clouds like the sky's big tears. Maybe stood, trying to get her breath back – breathing in and out in raggedy snatches as if her breath were a shirt caught on a thorny branch. In, out. In, out. She tried to calm down. In, out. She wished she would grow up, like *now*. Get the heck out of childhood. Much later she wondered, guiltily, if she had brought the whole thing on herself, if it was all the fault of that stupid wish. Because that night, before the barn dance had even taken place, before the harvest had finished, Molly MacPherson's childhood did indeed die.

But now, in the distance, she saw her mother's navy-blue car driving towards her, the windscreen wipers waving a frenzied greeting.

5

Jamie's Promise

'What's the matter with you?' Irene asked Maybe as she drove home fast round the country bends. 'Your face is a picture.'

'Nothing,' Maybe said, moodily.

'It's not the end of the world, you know, missing the school bus. I've forgiven you,' Irene said generously.

'Thanks,' Maybe said. 'Big of you.' Her voice was low and her face was glum.

Irene sighed. 'I'm sorry I was short with you. You caught me at a bad moment.'

'It doesn't matter,' Maybe said. 'Forget about it.' It was on the tip of her tongue to tell her mother about the Tongs, but she was too late. They had already turned down the muddy farm road, and her mum was on about what she was going to wear that night.

They went into the kitchen through the porch with the smelly wellies. They took off their wet coats and hung them on the coat hooks. The porch was steamy from the rain. A bucket of milk stood by the door.

They didn't ever need to buy bottles of milk; they took it fresh from the cows. Filled the bucket whenever they needed it. Maybe always drank a glass of milk as soon as she came home, and now she wiped her lips so as not to leave a milk moustache. Something was cooking slowly on the old Aga. 'What's for dinner?' she asked.

'Stew,' Irene said. 'I made it earlier.'

Maybe groaned. 'I thought we were having pasta.'

'Don't start, Maybe,' Irene said. 'We're going out.'

'I just said, I thought we were having pasta. How's that stopping you going out?' Maybe asked.

'Look, Molly, don't be cheeky,' Irene said. The only time she called Maybe by her proper name was when she was mad at her. The only time Maybe was cheeky was straight after an encounter with the Tongs. Maybe couldn't help herself. She turned sour and sullen, as if she'd been visited by a bad mood. There was nothing she could do about it. She felt the sulky face come on and sit on top of her own; she felt it freeze and take over. It was as tight as a mask and she couldn't pull it off. She couldn't smile.

'I hope you're not going into one of your sulks, Madam!' Irene said. Maybe hated being called Madam! Why did parents always have the knack of doing this? Calling you names that made you want to explode in fury?

'I'm not sulking. I just thought we were having pasta,' Maybe continued, rattled. If her mum was going to wind her up calling her 'Madam', then

Maybe would keep on saying, 'I thought we were having pasta,' until one of them broke down and screamed at the other and Irene's night out was ruined. Maybe saw her mother was upset and furious.

'Go ahead and ruin my evening!' Irene shouted.

Jamie came in from the milking in his red boiler suit. 'What's going on here?'

'It's Molly doing her usual,' Irene said, blinking back tears of rage.

'Calm down,' Jamie said. 'Come here, Maybe.'

Maybe rushed into her dad's arms. As soon as she saw him, she felt full of love for him and guilty about how she'd felt earlier when she'd wished he wasn't an Ibo.

'Hey?' he said, surprised. 'What's the matter?'

'Just give me a cuddle,' Maybe said, and Jamie held her. He looked accusingly over her shoulder at Irene. Irene looked back, furious. As far as she was concerned, Maybe had got her father wound round her little finger. Jamie was fair game for Maybe's machinations and manipulations; he was a big, gullible, handsome man.

'It's all over nothing at all, as usual,' Irene said. 'Madam here wants pasta, not stew.'

Maybe exploded. She couldn't keep it in any longer. 'Stop calling me "Madam". It's not that at all. That's not why I'm upset!'

Jamie put his hand up to stop Irene from talking. 'What is it?' he asked, gently.

'These kids at school keeping calling me "Ibo" and

things like that,' Maybe said, her head down. Irene's mouth fell open.

'You know Ibo is not a bad word, don't you?' Jamie said. 'You should be proud of being an Ibo.'

'They say it like it's an insult! They chant it,' Maybe said, her voice rising.

'Tell me their names!' Jamie said. 'I'll go to the school tomorrow and report them.'

'I don't want you to,' Maybe sobbed. 'That's why I haven't told you.'

'You mean this has happened more than once?' Irene asked. Maybe nodded. 'Oh, for God's sake. Why didn't you tell us? Come here,' Irene said. She patted the couch where she was sitting. Maybe sat beside her and Irene hugged her and said, 'I'm so sorry, Pet,' ruffling her hair.

'You weren't to know,' Maybe said, gulping between sobs. Everything already felt much better.

'Don't worry, Maybe, we'll sort it out,' Jamie said. He looked furious. The thought of anybody hurting his daughter's feelings made him want to draw blood. He was not a violent man, but he could wring the neck of anyone who hurt his daughter. He could stand his own feelings being hurt, but not Maybe's. It made him feel outraged and helpless.

'Is that why you missed your bus?' Irene asked, appalled, the thought having just occurred to her.

Maybe nodded, seriously.

'Oh, Maybe,' Irene said, upset now for shouting at her. 'Oh dear, dear.'

Maybe giggled a little. She was unable to take all the sympathy. She felt miles better now for having told them about the Tongs. 'You go and get ready for going out,' she said. 'Forget about it.' She felt magnanimous, mature.

Her father looked at her admiringly. 'That's the spirit. Don't let them break you. We'll sort the little spineless thugs out.' Jamie never insulted anybody. It was quite a thrill for Maybe to hear him say 'spineless thugs' with such hard contempt in his voice. 'I promise you, when I'm done, none of those thick rats will ever upset you again.'

Maybe laughed.

Jamie said, 'No, seriously. Look into my eyes. I promise you.'

Later, Maybe was to remember this scene almost word for word. As if the events that happened after it made her cling on to it, so that everything became painfully etched in her memory. She remembered her father's face, the look on it of love and determination. She remembered his bright, dedicated dark eyes. She remembered them always. For a moment she felt safe when he said it, full of trust. The future seemed brighter.

They sat around the table to eat Irene's chicken stew. The table was bright and colourful, with steamy bowls of greens and mashed potatoes and the big earthenware pot full of chicken and vegetable stew. 'It's really tasty, Mum,' Maybe said.

'Good,' Irene said, pleased. She drank a glass of red wine with her meal because she wasn't driving. Jamie ate his food very fast, shovelling big mouthfuls into his handsome face.

6

Night Out

Maybe could hear her mother humming a Beatles song, 'Eight Days a Week', as she got ready. She had one for practically every occasion. Maybe knew the words to most of the Beatles songs because Irene always sang them. There was a song for every feeling you had. 'Eleanor Rigby', 'The Fool on the Hill', 'Yellow Submarine', 'Lucy in the Sky with Diamonds', 'Yesterday'.

When Irene came down the stairs all dressed up to the nines, Maybe felt proud of her mother for being so good-looking. She was wearing a black skirt and a black top. She had a silver bangle on and bright red lipstick. She wore the earrings that Maybe had helped Jamie choose for her birthday last year. Long, dangly, silver things. 'What do you think?' she said putting a bright-green silk scarf around her neck. 'Wear it? Or not.'

'Not,' said Maybe. She loved giving her mother fashion advice because she always took it. Even when her father contradicted Maybe – even when he said, 'I like it on.'

'No, Maybe's the one with the flair for fashion, the style queen.'

Jamie was wearing his black jeans and a light-grey shirt. 'You look good too, Dad,' Maybe said.

'We try our best, don't we, sweetheart,' Jamie said, putting his arm round Irene and giving her a kiss. 'Is there a luckier man? I don't think so.'

'Don't stay up late with Annie. You need your sleep. By the time we're back, you'll be sound asleep.' Irene kissed Maybe on the forehead. 'And don't worry about those thugs. Your dad will see to them. There's Annie's car pulling up now, bang on time. Good old Annie.'

Maybe had known Annie all of her life. Annie did everything: she helped plough the land, milk the cows, tidy the house. She babysat whenever Maybe's parents went out. Annie was like part of the family.

It had already started to rain again. Maybe watched her parents' car drive down the bumpy farm road. She watched and watched till the tail lights disappeared off the end of the dirt-track road.

7

The Twins

Night-time. Wishing Well Farm. The rain pours down, pounding on the red farm roof, the corrugated iron barns, the muddy road. All of this will change. Wishing Well Farm is for the chop. As the rain lashes down, hard and fast, thudding like so many broken promises, the three men from the Property Development Agency (PDA) drive their black Mercedes down the A6Z6. The Mercedes has tinted windows. Nobody can see in, but they can see out. The dark, mysterious windows make you think of secrets, of plots, of danger.

'Is that Wishing Well?' Jimmy asked Harold.

Harold opened out his large Ordnance Survey map. The Barnes-Gutteridge brothers had never actually taken the trouble to visit over half of the land they owned. They had simply acquired it.

'Yep. That's Wishing Well. Well, well, in a couple of weeks there will be no more wishing for Wishing Well. If they refuse to listen to reason, they'll have to listen to force.' Arnold laughed. He had a sudden loud laugh that always startled people.

'I hope they *will* listen to reason,' Harold said. 'We need to get them off the farm before Domino will seal the deal. If the farm hasn't gone, Domino won't buy. We can't sell the land till we get rid of the tenants. It's our land, after all. Why should they be so difficult? They don't own the farm. We're offering them compensation.'

'Ah, but they love that farm, don't they?' Jimmy said.

'Well, we can't go bankrupt because they love the bloody farm,' Harold said.

'True,' Arnold said.

Harold and Arnold were identical twins. Harold was the older by six minutes. They were both very well-spoken and had been to boarding school. They came from a well-off Scottish family; their father owned several hundred thousand acres of land in the Western Isles. He had loaned them a considerable amount of money for various failed business ventures, and had now vowed not to part with a single penny more. They had purchased Wishing Well cheap and had always planned to sell it on for development.

Jimmy had a deep Glasgow accent. He was the Barnes-Gutteridges' handyman. They'd met him in a pub in Glasgow and got attached to him. When he'd told them he was out of work, they'd offered him a job. 'What will that involve?' Jimmy had asked.

'Practically everything.' Every job they did, every

place they went, they needed a handyman – a man who could turn himself to most small jobs, a bit of fencing, a bit of DIY, a bit of decorating.

'Well, I'm quite resourceful,' Jimmy had said. And he was as true as his words.

'Right then, I think we have a deal,' Harold had said. Jimmy drove back with them up to the Highlands. That was four years ago. Jimmy quite liked being their handyman, though he thought the twins were tight-fisted with their money.

Harold treated Wishing Well Farm to a large black X on the map.

'Bye-bye wee farm,' said Jimmy. 'Farms are stupit, anyway. No, boys?'

Harold and Arnold were still taken with the way Jimmy talked. They'd never had a handyman quite like him. Most of the people who worked for the brothers tried to speak politely, respectfully – at least in their presence. The cleaner, the gardener, the cook all spoke slowly and carefully in front of the brothers, never able to relax or be themselves, always aware that the brothers were their bosses, that the relationship was not equal. But Jimmy spoke to them the same way he spoke to everybody. With Jimmy, what you saw was what you got. He was not sly, not obsequious. He seemed not to care what people thought of him. The brothers respected him, and even looked up to him. They cared desperately what people thought of them, though they pretended not to.

'Oh, absolutely. Couldn't agree with you more,' Arnold said, winking at Harold.

Harold shone a powerful flash lamp on the farm. The screeching bright light illuminated the whole area for a couple of seconds. 'So we've given them notice, and if they don't shift we'll have to shift them – unfortunate but necessary,' Harold said, sighing as if the whole dreadful affair pained him.

'When is it again?' Jimmy asked.

'They've got three months from now.'

'That's generous,' Jimmy said.

Arnold laughed. 'That's one way of putting it. See those buildings over there?' he said. 'They'll have to be smashed into pulp to make way for the Domino Supermarket.'

'The family's name is MacPherson, by the way,' Jimmy said.

'MacPherson, MacPherson,' Arnold said rolling the surname round his tongue.

'What will they do with the coos?' Jimmy said.

'I guess they might slaughter them, or maybe another farmer will buy them. That's for them to sort out.'

'That won't be easy,' Jimmy said, whistling.

'That's life. You can't let things run down and fail and expect people to bail you out constantly. Why should I pay for their indulgence, tell me that?' Harold said angrily. 'The bloody MacPhersons believe in organic farming. They say that factory farming treats animals in a way that degrades the human beings as well as the animals, which is a bit rich.'

'That's right,' Arnold joined in. 'What was that their letter said? Oh yes, "Imagine forcing a woman to carry ten times more milk than she was meant to." ' Arnold laughed again. 'How idiotic to compare cows to people. I mean, cows just aren't people, are they?'

Harold went on, 'They said factory farm cows have their udders hanging with so much surplus milk they practically trail along the ground.'

'Is that right?' Jimmy said, trying to picture it.

'I'm sure they are exaggerating. These people are over the top,' Harold said.

'Aye, these people are right into their coos.' Jimmy loved discussing weird people.

'Well, it serves the MacPhersons right,' Harold said indignantly. 'Fancy thinking they could stand up to the might and mettle of the PDA. Let's face it bro', that farm is a run-down, dilapidated heap of old rubbish. They should have been bloody grateful for the PDA's generous offer.'

'Aye, well,' said Jimmy. 'They are for the smash soon. It will be Bye-bye MacPhersons, MacPhersons, Bye-bye.' He started to do a wee Bay City Rollers dance beside the Mercedes.

Jimmy revved up the engine and they shrieked off at a ferocious speed, singing to themselves. The twins joined in with Jimmy's song, 'Bye-bye MacPhersons, MacPhersons Bye-bye.' Only they pronounced it

MacFarsoon and that got to Jimmy. He didn't know why, but it got to him. He was really rattled. Driving off into the deep country dark, he thought again about the beloved cows being slaughtered. They whizzed past the dirt track that led down to the farm.

In her bed, Maybe tossed and turned and suddenly woke. She looked out of her bedroom window and could see nothing. It was still pitch-dark outside. She tucked herself back under her covers and fell asleep.

8

Maybe Grows Up Overnight

Two a.m. A police car arrived at Wishing Well Farm. A policeman and woman got out. Annie had been worried for the past hour and unable to settle. It was not like the MacPhersons to stay out this late. They were usually back by midnight at the latest. Annie heard the car coming down the farm track and peered out of the window. Her stomach turned over when she saw that it was a police car. She went to open the door.

Maybe appeared at the top of the stairs. 'Is that my mum and dad?' she asked. She hadn't been able to sleep for the past hour.

'Go back to bed, Maybe,' Annie said a bit sharply.

'There's no easy way to say this, so I'll get straight to the point. I'm afraid there's been a dreadful accident,' the policeman said. 'James MacPherson is dead.'

Maybe had been standing listening at the top of the stairs. She screamed and ran down. She rushed up to the policeman and pounded on his chest. 'I don't believe you. You're a liar. I don't believe you,' she shouted at him, sobbing and hitting him. The policewoman put her arm round Maybe, but Maybe wrestled out of her clutch. Annie took her in her arms and Maybe suddenly fell silent. She felt something inside her die. Her stomach felt empty and her mouth was completely dry. She felt her head go light and airy and her temples start to sweat and flame. She passed out.

Maybe came round, her head on Annie's lap on the sofa. She heard Annie saying, 'How is Mrs Mac-Pherson? Is she going to make it?'

'Yes, we think so. Apparently, all she has suffered is a broken leg, but she's very shocked. Car accidents are strange things. A matter of where you are sitting. You'll need to phone the hospital for more information. Do you want us to call your doctor out to give the girl a sedative?'

'No,' Annie said. 'She'll be OK with me.' Annie wiped the tears away from her face. Jamie Mac-Pherson was such a nice, kind man, she thought to herself. He was only in his middle thirties. Oh, God. Life! One minute somebody was here and the next they were not. How could it be?

The policewoman said, 'Don't get up, we'll see ourselves out. We're so sorry. So very sorry.'

Annie didn't know what to do next. Maybe was wideawake now. Annie went to the fridge and took

out some milk. 'I'm going to make you some Horlicks, love,' she said. 'To help you sleep.'

Maybe watched Annie stir the milk in the cup as
if she were doing it in slow motion. Annie stepped
towards her and handed her the mug. 'I'll need to
make some calls. You sip that and I'll be right back.'

Maybe heard Annie tell the news over and over
again. She called Fred first, her husband, to say she
wouldn't be home – that she would stay with Maybe
overnight. Maybe listened to Annie's soft, serious
voice and thought that they must have made a
mistake. Her father couldn't be dead. It wasn't possible: he had just this minute been alive. How could
you be alive and walking about in your lovely grey
shirt and black jeans one minute and dead the next?
How could you promise to sort out the spineless
thugs early in the evening and be dead by midnight?
Some mistake had been made. Her father was too
alive in her head to be dead.

When Annie came in from the hall, Maybe had
brightened. 'Annie,' she said eagerly. 'They've made
some mistake. My dad isn't dead.'

Annie's hands shook. She got up and poured
herself a whisky. Her eyes were full of tears. 'I'm
sorry, Maybe, but it is true. It's going to be hard to
accept, but it's true.'

Maybe felt herself sink again. Her mind wouldn't
stop. It was working fast and yet everything seemed
to be happening so slowly. Annie lifted her glass of
whisky to her mouth, sipped it, then put the glass

back down on the low table. She poured a little of her whisky into Maybe's Horlicks.

'I want to see my mum,' Maybe said. 'Take me to the hospital. I've got to see her. Even if I am just sitting by her side. I know she'll know I'm there. She'll sense me. She needs me. Take me, Annie, please.'

Molly, it's the middle of the night and your mum is injured. They won't let you into the hospital at night, sweetheart. You'll have to wait till the morning and try and get a bit of sleep. Snuggle down here with Annie.'

Maybe dozed in and out of sleep for a couple of hours. When she awoke, it was six in the morning. For a single glorious second she forgot the events of the night before. Then she remembered and felt sick to her stomach. She still could not believe it had happened. She couldn't believe her father was not going to walk in through that door and ask her if she was ready to help with the harvest.

Annie was asleep beside her on the couch, her head back and her mouth open. Maybe shook her awake. 'You have to drive me to the hospital, Annie,' she said, her voice tight with urgency. 'We have to go now.'

In the frail early-morning light, Maybe and Annie climbed into Annie's small car and drove up the bumpy farm road and through the lanes until they met the main A6Z6. Rain was lashing down. Annie's windscreen wipers waved, back and forth, back and forth. Maybe felt as if she had been gutted, like a fish – as if all her insides had been removed and discarded. Her limbs were long and aching, as if her bones had grown in the middle of the night. She didn't feel like a child any more. She felt old already. Her father's sweet and handsome face kept flashing before her. She could see him wearing his grey shirt, looking dashing and optimistic.

Annie drove along at a slow speed. Maybe was about to tell her to hurry up and then stopped herself. Annie was gripping the steering wheel for dear life. She couldn't think of anything to say and had never been one for talking for the sake of filling a space, a silence. Today, though, she would have given anything to be a talkative person. Her chest was tight, constricted. The girl in her charge was brave and silent. Not a word cracked out of her mouth. At the traffic lights, Annie took her hand off the gear lever and squeezed Maybe's hand.

'It'll not be long now,' she said. Then she said, 'Oh dear, oh dear, oh dear, oh dear,' because she couldn't help herself.

Maybe couldn't remember ever being in a hospital before. The long, arched corridors scared her. Endless corridors with frightening signs: Cardiology, Ortho-paedics, Maternity, Ear Nose and Throat, Radiology, Intensive Care.

Annie took Maybe through to the orthopaedics ward 10A. The nurse was friendly, almost as if she didn't know what had happened. 'Here to see your mum, are we?' she said and took Maybe's hand. Maybe looked at each bed expectantly. Strange patients stared at her passively as she walked by. Her eyes took in a bottle of Lucozade, a bowl of fruit, a jug of water, a leg in traction, a pair of eyes staring out from a bandaged head. A tall oxygen cylinder; a woman breathing through a mask. All of it appeared like something in a nightmare. Finally, she reached her mother. Her mother's face was not damaged, but her eyes stared at Maybe in an odd way, as if they were dead to the world and hardly able to take Maybe in.

Annie rushed forward. 'Oh, Irene,' she said, taking Irene's hand in hers. She told Maybe to sit down on the chair by the bed. Maybe took her mother's other hand and the three of them stayed like this for an age, like a still life, like something tragic somebody had painted.

Some time passed before a nurse came in and said, 'I'm sorry, you'll have to go now, she is still in shock and needs rest.'

Maybe looked into her mother's dead eyes. They hardly flickered. In that awful white moment, when her mother's cheeks were as white as her hospital sheets, Maybe felt that she had lost both her father and her mother to that wild night, to that heavy harvest rain.

On the way back to the farm, Annie managed a

whole couple of sentences. 'She'll not be like this for too long. It's the shock.'

But Annie was wrong. It was a long, long time before the light shone again through Irene MacPherson's eyes.

9

Irene Returns Home

A week later Irene MacPherson arrived back home. She climbed slowly out of Annie's car and walked around the side of it on crutches. She had broken her left leg – a serious fracture, tibia and fibula – but it would mend soon enough. The large, hard, white plaster cast made Irene look as if she was half human and half robot. But it was her broken heart that worried Maybe. Her mother's voice was low and flat. She sounded like a small child learning to read. She spoke slowly. 'I don't – think – I – can – do – this,' she said to Annie, struggling with her crutches. The sun shone over the farm. The sun could be cruel, callous, thoughtless. How could the sun still shine when Jamie MacPherson was dead?

Annie helped Irene to sit down on the sofa. She put a footstool underneath Irene's broken leg. Annie had thought it would be nice to have some relatives and friends there for Irene's homecoming, but Maybe had insisted they cope on their own. She was probably right. Irene didn't look as if she could cope with anybody else being there.

'Perhaps we should give up the farm,' she said, her voice thick and slow with sadness. 'What's the point now?'

Maybe, who had grumbled about the farm for much of her life, now felt passionately attached to it. 'You can't do that!' she shouted. 'Dad wouldn't have wanted that.' Staying on and looking after her cows and land was the only reason worth living for. It made her feel close to her dad.

Sometimes Maybe was sure she saw him watching over her, approving. She was sure that the cows missed him. They had been making more noise than usual and shifting anxiously from hoof to hoof, their big heads swivelling around as if to look for him. Maybe had told the cows point blank: 'He is not coming back. Look, there's no easy way to say this,' she had said to Birthday. 'He's dead. He's actually gone and died on us.'

It seemed to Maybe like an incredible fiction; she still could not believe in this strange new world – a world without a dad in it. It didn't have any hooks. There was nothing to hold on to. She peered down the old well and threw a coin in, squeezing her eyes shut. She knew she couldn't wish for her father to come back from the dead, because people didn't do that – just walk through the village, suddenly alive again – unless they were somebody in the Bible. If he could walk down the farm road and into the barn wearing his red boiler suit, he would. If the dead did allow him for one day to return to the living world, he would come straight to Wishing Well Farm. It didn't seem too much to wish for – her father coming back for one day only – but Maybe was too old to wish even for that.

She firmly believed in only wishing for what was possible. So she wished her mum would come back from wherever she had gone. Although her mother lived on the farm, it didn't seem like she was there at all. Her mind was faraway. Perhaps the driver that took her father's life also took her mother's mind. It seemed that way to Maybe. She peered down the well and whispered, 'Bring my mum back.' But she heard her own voice echo, *back, back, back*.

It was a grey day. Maybe was glad of the rain. She wanted to be the weather, to look how she felt. She walked beside her mother into the local crematorium. The minister talked about a man she didn't recognize as her father. It was difficult to believe that her dad was actually lying inside that coffin. If she could only pull back the lid and peer into his face one last time, then she might believe it.

Maybe and her mother were sitting on the front row. Maybe held her mother's hand. Irene's face was blank. The curtains closed on Jamie MacPherson. Maybe made her mind think of something else. She had been told what happens at cremations but she tried to put it out of her head. She pushed the whole thing back, back. But a flicker of a flame leapt right out of her imagination and licked at her face.

She sobbed out loud. Irene put her arm round her and held her. Her daughter's sobs seemed to waken her out of her deep sleep for a moment; and for a moment, Maybe took comfort in her mum's arms round her shoulders, holding her close. Irene wiped Maybe's tears with her fingers. Maybe cried more. It was the first time since her dad died that she had properly cried. You imagined you might cry all the time if something like this happened to you. The strange thing was, you didn't. You didn't cry as much as you needed to cry. You hardly cried at all. The tears froze inside you and it was a long time before the ice melted.

People understood tears. They didn't understand the stony face at a funeral – the face that looks as if it feels nothing at all. But that is the face that feels the most. Maybe knew that now. She knew her mum was hurting too bad to cry. An odd expression perched on Irene's high-boned cheeks. Perhaps it was pride. Perhaps the raw grief that lay underneath the surface of her face was too intimate to expose. She pulled her scarf around her neck and held her head high.

Maybe could feel people looking at them. Whenever there is a tragedy, people sneak looks at those who are the worst affected. The dreadful drama of it all made Maybe too aware of herself for a moment. She could feel her own reactions being watched and she felt a bit like an actress. She overheard Mrs Fisher saying, 'That poor girl loved her father to death.' She felt important for a moment. She followed herself, walking down the aisle and outside, her eyes lowered. *That poor girl.* But something about the expression bothered her. 'Loved him to death.' Was that possible? Had she loved him too much? Was his death connected to her love? Maybe shook her head as she left the crematorium chapel. The dark-red curtains were closed.

Quite a few people came back to the farm for the wake, where Annie had laid out a fine spread of food and drink. Jamie was much admired in Grumbeg; everybody liked him. What a big amiable man he was. Everybody ate the food – the sandwiches and sausage rolls and crisps – hungry all of a sudden, as if eating confirmed they were not dead. Quite a few took a nip of whisky, then another nip, then another. Before long, people were telling stories of Jamie – the time when he did this, the time when he did that; things he'd said, times he'd made them laugh. For a moment it felt to Maybe as if she had got him back, and she listened to the anecdotes with her ears stiff and alert as a dog's. The stories made her see pictures of him, made him move and turn and talk and laugh. The stories made him live again, just for a minute, a precious minute. There he was, suddenly ahead of her, laughing in the combine harvester. There he was, shouting down to her above the din as the combine cut the corn stalks right down, leaving only stubble, his face bright and animated, above his sky-blue T-shirt.

10

The Hairdresser

With the help of the farmhands, Annie and Fred, Maybe managed Wishing Well. Other local people had offered to help – the farmer down the road; Andy, the garage mechanic; Ms Rose, Maybe's teacher. But Irene turned down every offer. If they couldn't cope on their own, they would have to accept the compensation offer from the Barnes-Gutteridge brothers. Irene had always been a proud woman. Grief, it seemed, only intensified her pride. It wasn't possible for Irene to share her troubles or her sorrow. Maybe understood this, that the only people her mother could bear to see were herself, Annie or Fred. So every morning she got up at five o'clock for the morning milking before going to school. She helped Fred feed the cows, clean out their barn, milk them and lead them back out to the fields.

The herding was the most exciting. Maybe used her special herding crook and tried to see the cows not as separate animals but as one huge beast that she needed to move in the right direction. She led them like a conductor directing a big, rising piece of music – a crescendo with crashes and cymbals. The cows seemed to become part of a crowd when they were being herded. They moved flank to flank, swaying their sides back and forth, their tails circling the flies in one sweeping movement. They were a group of beasts moving as one. A big, stinking, swaying multitude.

Sometimes Maybe caught a glimpse of her father in the dairy. The back of his gentle head. His dark, soft, black curls straying down his neck in an unruly line. His dark neck. But then she looked up, and when she looked back he had gone.

There was so much to be done. The milk tanker arrived and Maybe supervised collecting the milk from the bulk tanks in the milking parlour. She worked the mill to make more barley feed. She drove the tractor and trailer up and down the fields along-side the combine harvester, the corn pouring into the trailer. Her father had died at the busiest time of year and all these jobs needed doing for the farm to survive. The cows needed bedding straw for the winter. She had been able to drive a tractor for ages, but she never used to drive without her father nearby, watching. Now, she did it on her own. Up and down her land. She knew the fields as intimately as her old dolls' faces. She had no time for dolls any more. They sat along the side of her room, wearing a sad, ignored look, their dainty little faces disappointed.

Exhaustion made Maybe's school work suffer. She was always behind at maths and English. She couldn't get a handle on long division. She could never work out the maths problems: if a man goes to the super-market and buys a box of eggs for £1.10, eight oranges for 15p each and a loaf of bread for 62p, how much change would he have from a five-pound note? Longitudes and latitudes were impossible to fathom. She couldn't retain the meaning of new words. Her spelling was shocking. One day she forgot to change into her school shoes and arrived at school wearing her big, green, farm wellies. Cow dung in the classroom. 'Miss, there's a strange smell in here!'

Ms Rose took pity on Maybe and turned a blind eye when Maybe fell asleep on her desk, resting her tired head on her arms. Of course, interfering Ina Doogle would always be sure to whisper fiercely, 'Ms Rose, I think Molly MacPherson has fallen asleep!'

'Oh, do you now, Ina Doogle, and what should make you think that?' Ms Rose said.

'I can hear her snoring, Miss,' Ina Doogle whispered.

The class all laughed loudly and Maybe woke up with a start. She rubbed her eyes and tried to look attentive. Then she noticed that everybody was staring at her.

School was a world that dealt in stares, like a kind of foreign currency or gambling chips. If stares did not exist, then school would be a different universe. It was the bloodcurdling stares of the Tongs that got to her, the slow stares that stuck to her back as she walked away. Not to say that Maybe didn't have friends, she did. She had three good friends – Violet, Gillian and Kirsty – but since her father's death, Maybe just didn't feel they understood how she felt. And when it came to defending her against the Tongs, they were nowhere to be seen. They were too scared. They watched their own backs. They never intervened if anybody called Maybe names. They shuffled their feet and looked embarrassed. Maybe preferred to be completely alone when she was being insulted – that way she didn't have to feel humiliated before her friends or suffer the double whammy of her friends letting her down.

In the past, Maybe's home cheered her up if school was bad. Not now. The threatening letters kept coming from the PDA and Maybe ignored them, throwing them on to a pile on the sideboard. She never showed them to her mother who was out of it still, listless, lifeless and lethargic. She wore her dressing gown till late in the day. She didn't bother to wash her hair. She never did the dishes. She had gone from being a very neat person to a total slob. Fancy having a mother who was a slob. It was not real. Children were meant to be the slobs, not mums. Yesterday, Maybe had gone into her mother's bedroom and was shocked at the state it was in.

'Look, Mum, you're going to have to tidy this mess up. I can't do everything,' Maybe had said. 'Do you realize how long it takes me to do the washing, and you just dump your things on the floor? If you don't put things away in your laundry basket, you're going to have to do your own washing and ironing,' and Maybe had banged her mother's bedroom door shut. Yes, her mother was grieving. But wasn't Maybe grieving too?

'I'm the girl here,' Maybe muttered to herself. 'I'm the one that is only eleven going on twelve who has lost her father.'

The phone rang. Maybe answered. It was Isabel Aird offering to come and cook dinner. 'Tell her we're managing,' Irene said. She couldn't face anybody. She didn't want to see a single soul.

Twice, Maybe had found food left in the front porch. Jeanette Cochrane left a lovely deep apple pie. Isabel Aird left a batch of rock cakes in a Tupperware box. Maybe showed them to her mum. 'That's nice,' Irene said, barely interested.

One day Maybe said to Irene, 'I'm going to shampoo you. I can't stand to see your hair in such a state.'

Irene said, 'Leave my hair alone.'

'It's needing washing. It's getting washed.'

Maybe led her mother by the hand to the bathroom where she made her sit in a chair and put her head back like she'd seen them do in the hairdressers. Then she stood at the side of the basin (pity she couldn't get right round to the back of it, like the ones they had in the salon) and scrubbed at her mother's scalp.

Irene had a lot of hair – long and red. Maybe's fingers massaged purposefully, making the shampoo lather up, all white and foamy like whisked egg whites. She rinsed the hair out, using a plastic jug. Then she squeezed it till she could hear it yelp and shriek, making that squeaky-clean sound.

'Now I'm going to blow-dry you,' Maybe said firmly.

'I don't want a blow-dry, Molly. Leave me now. My hair's done.'

'Nope. It's a blow-dry for you or else I'll invite people round for Sunday lunch.'

Irene conceded immediately. She hated seeing anyone these days, even Annie and Fred now. She went upstairs the minute she heard them come in. The only person she could bear was Maybe and, to be quite honest, even her own daughter's company was jarring. Irene simply wanted to be on her own for a very long time, perhaps forever.

She sat now on the straight-backed wooden chair, with Maybe on her tiptoes behind her, wielding the hairdryer. Irene's hair blew in every direction like her thoughts, like her life, like her dreams at night.

'Too much electricity in your hair, Mum. You could power things with that amount.' Irene managed a tiny tight smile. Maybe noticed it flicker for a second, new to her face. It was better than nothing, that mean, wee smile.

When Maybe had finished, Irene's hair was big and frizzy and she looked even more mad than she had when it was dirty. 'I just can't win,' Maybe said, disappointed. 'You'll have to learn to do it for yourself again.'

Maybe held up the hand mirror for Irene to take a look at herself. She could see her own face behind her mother's, her black curly hair behind the frizzy red.

11

The New Arrival

The morning light spilled across the fields, making the brown earth look red and the green grass glow. Maybe was walking across the barley field, taking long steps in her green boots. The song her father was teaching her before he died played in her head. She wished she'd learned it all now; of course she did. Wished more than anything that he had lived to hear her sing that African folksong: *Leave your hoes and dance with me*. Titi chom.

In her hand was a bucket of goose feed. She sprinkled it round the old well. If she had sung that song, she thought, he would still be alive. It was a terrible thought. She was the one who wished he wasn't an Ibo, who wished he didn't sing that song. She was the one who was embarrassed by him. And now he was gone. And it was too late, too late. *Leave your hoes and dance with me*. Titi chom.

She peered down the old well and shouted, 'Is anybody down there?' She threw in a penny and wished for a best friend – a friend who would really understand her. Her last wish hadn't come true yet; her mother was still absent. Perhaps this one would come true. Maybe it would, maybe it wouldn't. No, this wouldn't come true either. 'As if!' Maybe said aloud in disgust and stomped off to the barn to rip down the balloons and streamers, still up for the barn dance that had never happened. She got out the pitchfork and stabbed the hay again and again in fury. Stab. Into you. Stab. Got you. Take that. *Stab. Stab. Stab.* She was wild, sweating, fierce.

'OUCH!'

Suddenly, out of the plain gold hay, a girl made entirely of straw appeared.

'OW! OW! OW!' The girl made a strange sound; she had an odd, scratchy voice. For once in her life, Maybe was completely silent. She could not believe her eyes. She stared at the girl, unable to form a word in her mouth. The straw girl clutched at her side, dramatically. 'Ow!' she said again, tilting her large head.

Maybe laughed. 'It wasn't that bad. Come on, you're putting it on now. Is this a show?'

Strawgirl put her hands up in the air. 'No show,' she said, seriously. 'No show, Maybe.'

Strawgirl sat down. Maybe's eyes were out on stalks. She didn't know what was most surprising. For one thing, Strawgirl felt pain; for another she arrived straight after the wish; for a third thing, she knew Maybe's name – her special family name, not her official name.

Strawgirl was stunning. She was a solid shape made of thick straw – a golden yellow colour. She wore absolutely nothing except a red tartan kilt that was half-pulled on over her straw. It didn't fit properly and looked stuck on the straw like clothes stuck on a tree. 'Look,' she said to Maybe, pulling at the label on the back of her kilt, swivelling herself around awkwardly.

Maybe read, '*Hayley Rebecca Paterson. Who is she?*' Maybe asked. Strawgirl shrugged. Her black eyes were bright and mysterious; they shone like coal down a mine – like jewels.

'How do you know my name?' Maybe asked Strawgirl. She was thrilled out of her tiny mind. The pleasure she felt was so intense, the roof of her head could have flown open and three beautiful birds soared out.

'I know,' Strawgirl said, casually.

Maybe hoped against hope that she was not dreaming, that she would not wake up in a minute with Strawgirl gone.

'Help,' Strawgirl said honestly. 'Help farm. Fight enemy.' Strawgirl certainly didn't mince words.

'What enemy?' Maybe asked, excited.

'The same men.'

'Who?' Maybe didn't have a clue what she was talking about.

'First. Farm, dirty, let clean. Cow more milk. Paint house.'

'I can't do all that!' Maybe protested. 'I'm just

63

hanging on here by my fingernails. My mum's depressed, and we can't afford more help.'

'Only me,' Strawgirl said, and offered Maybe a bit of herself – of her own straw – as if she believed she was all that was needed. 'Only me,' she said again. A bird landed on a beam.

'First, play!' Strawgirl said. She closed Maybe's eyes with her scratchy hands. When Maybe wasn't looking, Strawgirl stripped off her kilt and left it on a bale. She was glad to be out of it. 'One, two,' she said to Maybe so that she'd know to count. Strawgirl had only worn the kilt so she would appear more normal to Maybe, more like an ordinary girl. Now she saw that Maybe liked her, she didn't need clothes. She wouldn't wear it again. The kilt hurt her straw.

She bounced up the big bales till she got to the top as Maybe counted aloud, 'Eight, nine, TEN, coming to get you, ready or not!' Maybe dashed around the barn. She looked everywhere. Suddenly she spotted Strawgirl's kilt. She pounced on it. Nothing doing. No Strawgirl! The cunning straw creature was naked! Maybe climbed up the bales to the top. Suddenly the bale that she stood on unravelled and Strawgirl bounced to her feet.

'That's not fair!' Maybe exclaimed. 'You can camouflage yourself. How can I hide from you?'

'Be not seen!' was Strawgirl's advice. She covered her bright eyes with her straw hands. One, two, three.

Maybe scrambled around the barn, searching for places to hide. She found a gap between two piles of bales. She squeezed into the middle and held her breath. It was hard not to just let your breath out in one raggedy gasp. She waited and waited to be found, but was not found. Maybe started to get anxious: it was better being the hunter than the hunted. It was lonely just hiding and waiting like this. For all she knew, she might never be found. For all she knew, Strawgirl did not exist. The golden sun shone into the barn. The birds twittered outside. A hen walked near Maybe on its dainty, tiny, pointed feet, shaking its big bottom of feathers. The back of Maybe's head itched. She put out her hand to scratch it and felt some straw sticking into it.

Strawgirl sang triumphantly, 'Here!' like a bell ringing. 'Here. See not seen,' she said.

Maybe didn't understand half of what Strawgirl said, but it didn't seem to matter. 'I didn't like it,' she said. 'It was too long. I thought I'd never be found.'

They went outside to climb the trees. Strawgirl stood beside a beech tree with its smooth bark and whistled up a wind. All her straw blew up the tree, and when it got to the top it looked like a branch. She swayed with the other branches from side to side. Maybe couldn't see Strawgirl until she sat up.

'Olo!' Strawgirl shouted down. 'Olo!'

Maybe scrambled up the tree. She had always been a good and devoted tree climber – sure-footed, brave, adventurous. They sat together, surveying the farm, the fields empty now of wheat and barley since the harvest was brought in. They could see the stationary red tractor, the rabbits, the late roses, the rare birds.

'Look!' Strawgirl pointed to a bird, almost level with them.

'It's a red kite!' Maybe said. She had only ever seen one once before, with her father, a year ago.

Strawgirl could barely pass a tree without wanting to climb it. Once up, high in the branches, she seemed to grow greener and disappear among the leaves. Her eyes turned the colour of crab apples or hazelnuts, and Maybe had to stare hard to make her out among the foliage. Like Maybe, Strawgirl loved to hug trees if she was sad. Maybe could feel the tree's kindness and wisdom against her body – feel the sap healing her sore blood.

Maybe climbed down the beech tree, and Strawgirl swirled down, whipping up a wind. She looked like a straw whirlwind, spinning yellows and creams and browns. 'Skip!' she shouted.

Maybe had not had so much fun for a long time. 'I haven't got a skipping rope,' she said.

'Skip!' Strawgirl said, and unravelled a bit of her arm to make a rope. Maybe gasped and took one end of Strawgirl's extended arm while Strawgirl took the other. They both skipped, jumping over the long straw rope at the same time.

Strawgirl grabbed Maybe's hands and made her dance with a silver birch, round and round and round. Strawgirl stood beside the trees and tilted her head to one side. 'Listen!' she said. For the first time,

Maybe heard the trees' language; the leaf-whisper, the branch-creak, the twig-snap, the trunk-groan were all part of tree vocabulary. Trees could sing, particularly when it was windy. Trees could gossip – that was what they were doing when rain pattered through their leaves. Trees could even tell jokes by sending birds cackling from one tree to another. Sometimes Strawgirl would stop dead in Maybe's forest and burst out laughing at a punchline that had just flown overhead from pine to pine. Maybe understood that if you hurt a tree, you hurt the spirit of life itself.

Maybe would have never believed it – Strawgirl was a wish come true. Why had the wishing well finally listened? Was it because she was grieving? Because she was so painfully sad? She had got her best friend. All right, she was made of straw. But still. She was the most unusual, enterprising, original, surprising, particular best friend any girl in the whole of the Highlands could wish for. Make that the whole of the Lowlands too. The whole of Scotland – no, in the whole of the UK; no, in the whole of single-currency Europe; no, in the whole of the Northern Hemisphere; no, in the whole of the world . . . in the galaxy, in the vast expanse of space and universe. That was it. Strawgirl was the best friend a girl could have out there.

That first night, Maybe fell asleep in her bed, happily exhausted, snug under her covers while Strawgirl slept in the barn – hay on hay, straw on straw, indistinguishable under the moonlight. The moon was split in two, so cleanly that you couldn't help imagining the moon's missing half.

12

Cull Castle

Cull Castle lay far back from the winding road at the top of the hill. It stood in its own grounds which extended from Cape Wrath to the Dornock Firth. One thousand, seven hundred and thirty-five square miles. A forest of tall Scots pines surrounded the castle, the trees like wooden sentries on duty, standing to attention. A glimpse of the old stone fortress and its turrets could be caught through the dark trees. The windows were still tiny from the days when windows were designed to protect the royal blood inside. Few visitors these days ever came near Cull Castle. It was not open to the public. The National Trust had not bought the land. No, the land still belonged to the Barnes-Gutteridge brothers.

The twin brothers lived and worked inside the castle. They ran their business, the Property Development Agency, from a large room on the ground floor. In their office, there were three computers, a photocopier, several large filing cabinets, an in-tray and an out-tray, an office planner and an office diary, where the brothers systematically wrote down dates of appointments. Each brother had his own large desk in the office. Arnold's desk was always exceptionally tidy, every paper put away at the end of the day. Harold's was messy: pens, papers, letters, old envelopes, notes, phone numbers, empty coffee mugs, paper clips, CDs, bank statements and floppy disks lay strewn all over it. There were several false tax claims, bogus expense forms and examples of undeclared income lying on his desk. Harold thought nothing of cheating to make more money. He was involved in more than one underhand deal. It gave Arnold a headache just to look at his brother's desk so he often averted his eyes. There was no changing Harold. Harold had messed up their bedroom when they were boys, then he'd messed up their dormitory in boarding school, and now he was messing up their castle. Arnold had once heard somebody say, 'Show me the boy and I'll show you the man.' He fervently believed it. They were both still the same. Yet Harold was the brother with clout, despite being a messy son of a gun.

If you did just happen upon the castle at Cull, you would feel uneasy, you would shiver, shake or shudder. It seemed to exist on the edge of a world of its own. On bright days, the sun did not reach the grounds. On days when it rained in other parts of the Highlands, it hailed and snowed at Cull. A thin mist at Wishing Well Farm was a dense, thick, eerie, dangerous fog at Cull. A thick pea-souper fog could last for four days without ever lifting. The winds lashed and tore at the stoical pine trees, at the west wing and east wing of the castle. Inside the long, damp corridors, the wind would find its way in. Paintings were always falling down. Newspapers blew along the hall. At night, the desperate howl of the wind could have woken the dead.

The brothers loved their castle. 'It's terribly idiosyncratic, isn't it?' Harold said to Arnold when they first bought it.

'Absolutely,' Arnold said and gulped with laughter, seeming to swallow every second giggle, his thin shoulders shaking like a wire coat hanger on a washing line.

They had dreamed about owning a castle when they were boys. When they grew up they were surprised how easy it was to acquire one. A large loan from their father, a manageable mortgage and that was it.

Arnold and Harold were both tall, thin, reedy men with blond fly-away hair. Most people couldn't tell which one was which. If you knew them very well, you could easily see that Arnold had a higher forehead, shaped like a dome. His nose was slightly sharper and his eyes slightly smaller. He was forever putting his hand to his forehead and running his hair back to keep it in place. But damn it if it didn't just flop forward again. He had full, tender-looking lips, always too moist. Harold's lips were always dry and his mouth closed tight unless he was talking. Arnold had a nervous disposition, whereas Harold was more confident and arrogant. Arnold often felt that he wouldn't survive without his twin. Harold often wished he could shake his twin off him; Arnold clung to him like a leech, like a bloodsucker. Harold was irritable; Arnold tried to please.

Jimmy could tell the brothers apart now without any effort. He preferred Arnold to Harold, but wished Arnold would stand up for himself more. Jimmy was a good deal smaller than the twins. He had dark, curly, short hair and was stoutly built. His brown eyes were bright with mischief. If you had known Jimmy when he was a boy, you wouldn't have thought he had changed all that much.

As well as owning the land occupied by Wishing Well Farm, the twins owned two other farms – Holly Farm and Red Road Farm. Here was the plan. The brothers' Property Development Agency would sell each of its three farms to make way for new developments. The first on the hit list was Wishing Well Farm. That deal was pretty close to completion. What they needed was the land to be free of the MacPhersons and their cattle and then they could proceed with demolishing the farm buildings. They could then sell the land on to the Domino supermarket chain. The problem was the MacPhersons themselves who refused to jump and would therefore have to be pushed. The brothers might have achieved what they wanted legally if they'd hired some lawyers, but it would cost a lot of money and Harold hated spending money. It was their land, after all. If they wanted to sell it so a supermarket could be built to improve life for the local community and bring money to the area, that was their business. 'That's how the cookie crumbles,' as Harold said.

'Life is tough for the coo farmer, isn't it?' Jimmy said one evening over a bowl of soup. He was already having second thoughts about the whole business. If he hadn't desperately needed the money, he wouldn't be working for the twins.

Harold slurped his soup noisily, making his mouth into a Hoover and sucking it up. 'Without a doubt,' he said, in the middle of a big spoonful of Scotch broth. 'Unspeakably, unbearably, tough.'

'Those MacPhersons haven't responded to our fifth eviction letter. Do you think something is the matter?' Arnold asked, sipping quietly and neatly.

'Like what?' Harold said.

Well, do you think they can read?' Arnold said, laughing a little.

'Apparently there's been a death in the family,' Jimmy said.

'Well, if they haven't responded properly by the end of the week,' Harold said, 'we'll have to pay them a visit, death in the family or no death in the family.'

'How long does a funeral take?' Arnold asked.

'Not long,' Harold replied.

'They might have been having one of them nine-day wakes if the mother is Irish,' Jimmy said knowledgeably.

'Don't be stupid, Jimmy. Nobody has wakes any more. The man will have been cremated days ago. It's pure obstinacy, nothing more,' Harold said.

'Give it to the end of the week then,' Jimmy said.

'No more,' Harold said, cleaning the wax out of his ear with his finger and licking the back of his spoon. 'If they don't shift, we will have to think of some tactics to shift them.'

'Such as?' Jimmy asked.

'Well, they are fond of their cows,' Harold mused. 'We could steal a couple and threaten to slaughter them.'

'That wouldn't be nice for the cows,' Arnold said.

'Of course it wouldn't be nice for the cows! But bear in mind they're only beasts. Beasts don't feel pain like humans. You can only feel pain if you are an adult. Even children are not sufficiently sophisticated to feel real pain. Babies don't feel anything at all. They never used to give them any anaesthetic, you know, in the past, because they knew babies couldn't feel the operating scalpel. They just screamed to hear the sound of their own lungs.'

Jimmy didn't like any talk of hospitals. He was an extremely squeamish man; just the sight of blood made him want to faint. 'Spare the details, Harold, I'm eating my soup here,' he said, taking the bowl in both hands and drinking the dregs of the broth straight from it.

'By the time we finish with those cows, the Mac-Phersons will be wishing they had accepted the offer of compensation. Some farmers are just bonkers, Jimmy, bonkers. Mad cows and mad farmers. What a world.'

'Any chance of some more broth?' Jimmy said.

Arnold got up and peered into the soup pot. 'It seems to have congealed,' he said.

'Turn the heat back on,' Harold said, irritably. Arnold turned the gas on high and added some water, too much water.

'You daft idiot!' Jimmy said staring bleakly into the big pot. 'I dinny like ma soup all watery.'

13

Strawgirl Gets to Work

Maybe woke up at dawn, ready for the morning milking. All night she had dreamed of Strawgirl and prayed that she was not just an apparition. She pulled on her old milking clothes and tiptoed down the stairs so as not to wake up her mother (who seemed to spend most of her days and nights sleeping). In the porch, she put on her green wellington boots and her bright-red boiler suit over her old clothes. She rushed outside. The sun was just rising shyly in the sky, a bit flushed, blushing. Maybe dashed to the barn.

She could not see her. She felt an aching, bitter disappointment. She was just about to cry when the straw at the back of the big barn moved and sat up. It was Strawgirl! Arisen. Awoken. Up. Moving. It was she! She was real!

Maybe had forgotten how the bales were Strawgirl's camouflage – exactly her colour and texture. Asleep, she became them.

'Good sleep,' Strawgirl said, yawning. 'More!'

'That's how I feel every morning,' Maybe laughed. 'Oh, just to fall back, snug, and snuggle back down.'

Strawgirl hunted for her kilt and held it up. 'No like,' she confessed to Maybe.

'Do you want other clothes?' Maybe asked, suddenly excited at the idea of having to rustle through her wardrobe for clothes to suit a straw girl.

'No. No clothes,' Strawgirl said. 'No like.' She looked at Maybe for a long moment, waiting to see what she would say.

'Why did you wear the kilt then?' Maybe asked her.

'Maybe,' Strawgirl replied.

'For me?' Maybe asked.

Strawgirl nodded. 'Yes.'

It moved Maybe, the idea that her new friend had got all dressed up to meet her when she obviously never normally wore any clothes at all. 'This morning I was desperate to get up and come down here,' she said.

'Why?' Strawgirl said, hanging on to the 'y' so that it sounded like 'whyyyyyyy?' A bright smile burned in her coal-dark eyes.

'You know!' Maybe said, laughing appreciatively.

'No,' Strawgirl said, artlessly. 'Tell.'

'To see if you were real.'

'Real?' Strawgirl said, shocked, a little hurt.

'I didn't mean that,' Maybe said, confused. 'I really meant I was desperate to see you again.'

'Oh!' Strawgirl said. 'Me?' She smiled. Of course

she had known that all along. 'Now, cows,' she said to Maybe.

Into the barn they went. Strawgirl watched as Maybe herded the first eight cows into the milking shed. Each cow walked calmly to her proper stall, her big behind swaying confidently. This morning, the milk spilled and spilled. There was five or six times the usual amount.

'This is amazing!' Maybe squealed. 'Has this got anything to do with you?'

'Me?' said Strawgirl. 'No, you.'

Maybe had thought the cows might be nervous in the presence of Strawgirl, for they were not brilliant with strangers, but she didn't bother them. Cows are sociable beasts. They liked it when Maybe sidled up to them and rubbed against their flank for a cow cuddle.

The cows' udders looked like bagpipes. Maybe was astonished when Strawgirl lent a helping hand and the milk flowed even faster. Strawgirl didn't even need to pull at the teats the way Maybe did with Scunnert. She simply pointed to them softly with her straw fingers and the milk came. Most amazing of all: when Strawgirl milked Scunnert, music came out of her teats, just as if she were playing the bagpipes! Maybe recognized a couple of songs – Burns songs. 'For a That' and 'John Anderson My Jo' poured enthusiastically into the silver bucket. So did 'My Father Was a Farmer.' Maybe found herself singing along as she pulled the musical teats.

*'My father was a farmer upon the Carrick
   border, O*
And carefully he bred me in decency and order, O
*He bade me act a manly part, though I had ne'er
   a farthing, O*
*For without an honest manly heart, no man was
   worth regarding, O.'*

'Strawgirl? How do you do that?' Maybe asked in awe.

'Want blues?' Strawgirl said.

'That's funny, my dad liked the blues and jazz.'

'Yes,' Strawgirl said as the sun reached higher up in the sky and streaked through the barn doors, lighting up the milk in the pails, the cows' tails, the old wooden stalls. This glorious morning seemed blessed by the light, like a golden message from somebody special.

Maybe pulled hard on The Empress's teats and 'St Louis Blues' started playing. It had been one of her father's favourites along with 'St James Infirmary Blues'. Maybe didn't know whether to laugh or cry.

'How did you know that?' Maybe asked sharply.

'Gift,' Strawgirl said. 'Dad, sad.' A tear rolled down her face.

'Oh, my God! You can cry!' Maybe said, dipping The Empress's teats in disinfectant solution.

'Yes,' Strawgirl said. 'And wee-wee.'

'You can't!'

'Yes!'

Maybe looked on, appalled and thrilled, as Strawgirl squatted down and peed outside the milking shed. It was a long pee and the heat from it rose like steam. 'Wow!' Maybe said, impressed.

'Do you? Do you . . .?' Maybe couldn't finish her question.

'Poo? Yes, but no for Maybe,' Strawgirl said. 'Poo's pooey.' she sniffed the air.

It seemed Strawgirl knew everything about Maybe's herd of cows. She knew each cow's name. Somehow she had memorized all sixty-four of them.

There were four groups of sixteen cows. Cows liked to be kept in their particular group; they didn't like mixing with new cows or strangers. It made them nervous. It didn't help the milk flow. The only time they had to be separated was when some cows were dry and others wet. Then the dry cow had to be reintroduced to its herd after a couple of months. The cow didn't like that. She didn't like having to re-establish her place in the herd, like a child who returns from a long absence from school to find her best friend huddled in the corner with another girl.

The four herds' names were organized in themed groups. There was the Scottish group, the Blues and Jazz group, the Book group and Maybe's herd. Maybe had named her cows, but her father and mother had had lots of fun naming all the rest. Bertha, Crabbit, Sleekit, Torag, Lady Muck, Auntie Agnes, Haggis, Thistle, Tattie Scone, Irn-Bru, Stornoway,

Tartan, Hooch-the-Noo, Stromness and Scunnert were some of the cows in the Scottish group. The leader of the Scottish contingent was Stromness.

In every grouping of cows there is a natural leader: one who is first to go to graze, first to lie down, first to lead off for the twice-daily milking. There is also always a very dominant, bossy cow in each grouping, but she somehow never manages to be the leader. The other cows are too discerning. The bossy one in the Scottish contingent of cows was Thistle. She was always trying it on, bumping into other cows and trying to get first in the queue.

Ma Rainey, The Empress, Lady Day, Memphis Minnie, Ethel Waters, Dinah, Sarah, Ella, Cassandra, Nina, Odetta, Alberta and Little Laura were among the cows in the blues group. They were the slowest group of the lot, but they sure could swing their big behinds. The leader of this group of cows was Ma Rainey; The Empress was the bossy one who always tried to get the longest bits of grass and was often desperate for a bull to come and get her pregnant.

Wishing Well didn't use a bull these days. They used artificial insemination. It was quicker and more efficient and you didn't have to keep some bad-tempered, unpredictable bull in a pen all year round.

The third herd were named after writers or characters that the MacPhersons admired. There was Madame Bovary who was always off, trying to find new pastures. There was Zora, Anna Karenina, Scarlett and Jhabvala. Jane Eyre was an emotional cow with a plain face. Wuthering Heights hated storms and gales. There was Morrison, Mansfield, Munro, and Middlemarch. Middlemarch seemed to know everything about all the other cows. Then there was Plath, an erratic and imaginative cow that made patterns when she grazed. There was Sargasso Sea, a highly strung, nervous cow. Middlemarch was the leader of this herd, and Mansfield was the bully.

They finished the milking at record-breaking speed, with more milk to show for it than Maybe had seen in her young puff. 'I canny believe my eyes,' she said, her voice full of wonder and surprise. She would have liked to have 'gifts' like the ones that Strawgirl obviously had. How do you go about getting gifts? she wondered.

When they had finished the milking it was seven-thirty – time for Maybe to get ready for school, to have a quick shower, a bowl of muesli, an orange (high in vitamin C) and a teaspoonful of cod-liver oil. Her father used to insist on Maybe having this for her bones to grow, for her hair to shine, but she used to run a mile from the spoon. Since he had died, though, Maybe felt it was her duty to do things the way he wanted them done, in his honour. It was a terrible thought, but her father's death had turned her into a better person. She never used to have a sense of duty before. She wished that she had. She wished he'd been around to see it, to watch her grow up.

Now that her dad was dead, Maybe was interested

in everything to do with him. One day she wanted to save up and fly to Nigeria. She tried to imagine what her African grandmother would look like – if she'd be tall like Maybe's father or small. She tried to picture what their house was made of, whether they lived in a city or in the country. She imagined the land, the sky in the early light; she remembered her father talking of 'big African skies'. She wondered whether his family would like her, or whether she would just be too different, too Scottish. She wondered if anyone could ever have the same feelings as her. She wished she'd asked her father more about the Ibo – what they believed in, their customs and rituals, their traditions. Suddenly Maybe found herself consumed with interest. How she wished she hadn't been bored when her father had talked about Nigeria.

The cod-liver oil had a particularly nasty and distinctive taste that seemed to cloy and stick to the roof of the mouth. It was a green and vulgar taste, like poison from the bottom of a fishy pool. But Maybe endured it. She had a glass of orange juice at the ready to down swiftly after her spoonful. In a few months' time, she wouldn't even need that. She'd be hard by then.

Her school uniform – the pleated skirt, the grey jumper, the white blouse, the maroon-and-blue striped tie, the maroon blazer, the polished black shoes and grey tights – were all laid out waiting for her. Maybe stared at her bed, shocked. Her mum must be getting better, she thought. Mum's on the mend.

She rushed through to her mother's bedroom. Her mum lay staring at the ceiling. 'Thanks for laying out my uniform,' Maybe said.

'Do you have to be sarcastic?' her mum said and rolled over.

Maybe stared open-mouthed, and then she realized who had laid out her uniform. She smiled to herself and kissed her mum on the forehead. 'See you later,' she said cheerfully.

Maybe jumped down the stairs, taking two at a time. She was just about to start getting her packed lunch ready when she spotted her Tupperware box on the table. She opened it up: inside was a tuna and cucumber sandwich in a little sandwich bag, a strawberry fromage frais, a red apple, a blackberry health bar and a carton of apple and mango juice. On top of the drink was a little note in very scratchy handwriting: *For you, SG*.

Maybe walked to the end of the farm road with quite a bounce in her step. She didn't even feel as tired as usual because her spirits were high, high as a sparrow, a swallow, a starling. Which bird flies the highest? Maybe wondered. Since Strawgirl arrived she had started asking questions like this all the time. Strawgirl knew everything: she knew where the swallow slept, what the eagle ate, where the badger buried its mice, when the sycamore leaves got their spots, why the ferret chased the dog, why the stoat turned silvery white in winter, where the squirrel buried its acorns.

A robin appeared for a moment, with its puffed red chest, small and heart-warming. Then it disappeared under the hedge.

14

The Return of the Tongs

Maybe waited dreamily for the school bus. All of her thoughts were for her straw friend. Her mind was so far away that she hardly noticed the bus in the distance, rounding the bend and heading towards her. Maybe would have rather been at the farm with Strawgirl than at school. She learned more at the farm, anyway. When she grew up, she would run Wishing Well. She would never leave her farm. She loved it passionately now: the old farmhouse, the fields, the land, the cows, the barns and the hay. The way the light turned the whole farm to gold. Even the old dirt track leading down to it. Working on the farm since her father died had made her love it more. Perhaps it was a way of loving him; perhaps she had replaced him with the land.

The bus arrived at her school, and Maybe felt her heart sink. Only the secret and delicious thought of Strawgirl could cheer her up. During that day, she found her mind drifting off to dream about Strawgirl standing in front of her with an earnest expression on her straw face. Strawgirl had high, wide cheeks, which made her look rather beautiful.

The Tongs had lain low for a couple of weeks because they heard that Maybe's father had died and it made them nervous. But decent gangs can't stay idle for all that long and it was time to make the MacPherson girl pay. She owed the Tongs for the humiliation they had suffered the day of the kilt episode. 'Bide your time, big man,' Troy said to Moron. 'We'll get her today, after school. Just wait. She's got it coming.'

Ms Rose was doing a lesson about the blues. She asked the class if anyone knew anything about the blues tradition. Maybe's hand shot up. 'Yes, Ms Rose.'

'Go on, Molly,' Ms Rose said, pleasantly surprised. Molly was not one of her usual volunteers.

'The blues came out of the tradition of African folk music. The slaves, who had been taken from Africa to North America, sang slave songs and spirituals and work songs, and that music changed into early blues and then gospel and then jazz and then soul and now rap. W.C. Handy was the father of the blues. The first woman to make a blues record was Mamie Smith back in 1921 with 'Crazy Blues'. The blues singers had great names. Howling Wolf. Muddy Waters. Blind Lemon Jefferson.'

Maybe was breathless by the time she had finished. She had no idea where all this information was coming from; her father had taught her some of it, but she had never really listened properly when he was going on about blues and jazz. Now it just suddenly sprang from her mouth. Maybe had hardly made the effort to talk. It was as if the words were just waiting to be said, as if someone else had put them there.

Ms Rose was stunned. The whole class looked at Maybe admiringly. So things were looking up for her, at school and at the farm. That was until she walked towards the bus for the journey back home.

The Tongs were waiting behind the hedge before the bus stop. Maybe spied them and started to sprint. She ran so fast she alarmed herself; her own speed was scary. But this time they were not going to give up. Maybe jumped on the bus and they jumped on too. When it came to their stop, they didn't get off. Maybe turned round quickly to look at them. They were sitting in the back row, smiling at her; not a friendly smile at all – a nasty, cruel leer, curdled and violent.

When it was her stop Maybe jumped off before anybody else and ran for it – for dear life. But Troy, Moron and Spider were right behind her. They followed her all the way down her farm road. The dust and dry dirt blew in every direction. Nobody was around to see her. She ran fast, dodging all the potholes. She could see home ahead of her, but nobody appeared to be in the old farmyard except a couple of hens. She skidded on the muddy, cobbled yard and ran in to the barn. The boys were some distance behind her. Strawgirl was just waking up from her afternoon nap. Maybe climbed up the bales and sat beside her.

'They're after me Strawgirl,' she hissed.

Strawgirl sat bolt upright. 'Who?'

'The Tongs,' Maybe whispered. 'They're just out there.'

'Take tie off!' Strawgirl ordered. 'And blazer.' She threw Maybe's clothes over to the other side of the barn. Then she told Maybe to lie down flat, and she lay on top of her.

Suddenly the boys walked into the barn. They looked around and were about to go and look in the barn next door, when something caught Troy's eye. It was Maybe's school tie. 'Over here!' Moron shouted. He picked up the tie and the blazer. 'Look at this!' he said. 'She's been here. She's probably still in here.'

Strawgirl lay completely flat so Maybe couldn't be seen.

'Right, well, let's smoke her out,' Troy said. 'We'll set fire to a couple of these bales. That will get her running.'

Maybe wriggled out from under Strawgirl. She climbed down with her hands up. 'I give in,' she said. What do you want me to do?' She stood facing the boys. Somehow, having Strawgirl there made her bolder.

Troy had a box of matches in his hand. 'Put this

out,' he laughed, striking one of the matches and then using it to set alight the entire box. He threw the box up in the air, and it landed right next to Strawgirl. Maybe saw her rush along the top row of the bales of straw to the right side. The bullies didn't appear to have seen her. 'Let's just stay here for a minute and watch that fire take,' Troy laughed.

Maybe screamed, 'No!' She had to protect Strawgirl. She picked up a pitchfork and ran at Troy who backed off, running backwards.

'Steady on!' he shouted. 'You can't use weapons!'

'Why can't I?' she shouted back, jabbing him straight in the middle of the stomach with the pitch-fork. 'You've used matches.' She called the geese, ordering them to, 'ATTACK!' It was a command she had taught them but never given them.

They could hardly believe their goose luck. All their life they'd been longing to use their special guard-geese skills. They came running, flapping and honking. One of them pecked the back of Moron's leg. Another tripped Troy up while a third sat on his face and did a big goose special on his red cheeks. Spider had his face slapped by strong goose wings. The boys shouted in terror.

'Come on. Come on. Get out of here!' Troy said, wiping his face and trying to get up. He scrambled to his feet and staggered towards the barn door. Three vicious and vindictive geese chased him; the backs of his legs were tasty. Spider was crying, his face pale as the driven snow. Troy's face was red with rage. Moron blinked rapidly and was totally breathless.

'We'll get you another time, Molly MacPherson,' Troy shouted. 'You wait. Just you wait.'

Spider looked at Troy as if to say, 'You're on your own next time, pal. I'm no coming back here with these geese aboot the place.'

The Tongs ran off into the distance with the geese chasing them all the way up the farm path. Their honking sounded like hysterical laughter.

Maybe stamped on the fire to put it out. Luckily, it had not caught properly yet. Flames can spread like wildfire on a farm with all that dry straw.

Strawgirl was hopping up and down, anxiously. Maybe had never seen her look anything but radiant and optimistic. 'Fire!' Strawgirl gasped. 'Fire – no power.'

It was the first time Maybe had heard Strawgirl admit that she had powers. It filled her with a tremendous excitement. Having a good friend was wonderful; having a friend with special powers was stupendous.

Maybe wondered what Strawgirl's powers involved. 'What can you do?' she asked her.

'You'll see,' Strawgirl said, her confidence returning. 'Promise.' Maybe's eyes sparkled and shone, lit up by Strawgirl's strength.

The matches looked like small dead people – stick people with burnt heads. Maybe picked them up one by one and laid them on the palm of her hand. 'You didn't work,' she said to them. 'You didn't take off.' She took them into the yard and threw them in the bin. Outside, the sky cracked open and the rain came pelting down.

15

Bullying

Maybe knew that Strawgirl didn't really understand bullying. Bullying was a human thing, a person-to-person thing, and Strawgirl was a creature, not a person.

How could Maybe explain to Strawgirl that human beings called each other names and picked on each other because they were different? How could Maybe tell Strawgirl what 'Darkie' meant or 'Fatso' or 'Chinky'? When Maybe thought about explaining those insults to Strawgirl, the words themselves seemed alien, unbelievable, strange. When she considered telling Strawgirl that some people hate Muslims for being Muslims or Sikhs for being Sikhs or Catholics for being Catholics, it seemed preposterous, outlandish. Why would people behave like that to each other? Why would some people spit at other people, or hit them, or beat them up, or murder them because of their colour or their faith? Maybe felt embarrassed about it, ashamed.

Maybe could feel shame even though she was not

the one who was doing the bullying. She felt shame for the people who called her names because they were human, not creatures or even monsters. It didn't help her to think that they were 'animals'. They weren't animals; they were human beings. Human beings, children, filled with prejudice and hatred.

The Tongs had waited outside school for Maybe like they had done so many other days. They had called her vicious, nasty names. Sometimes they got hold of her and shoved mud in her mouth. Sometimes they told racist jokes.

'What do you call two darkies in a sleeping bag?' Troy would say.

'Twix,' Moron would say.

'What do you call a darkie committing suicide?' Troy would ask.

'Chocolate drop,' Moron would reply.

Other times they sang as Maybe walked past: 'Nuts! Oh, hazelnuts! Cadbury's take them and they cover them in chocolate.'

How could she explain that to Strawgirl? It was too complicated. It was too horrible. Maybe didn't actually want Strawgirl to find out about it. In a peculiar way, Maybe wanted to protect Strawgirl, so that she could safeguard her friend's innocence. There were some things you just didn't want your straw creature to know about. Some things you had better keep quiet about. The world was a scary place, full of hatreds. Strawgirl was full of love. Maybe knew that Strawgirl, if she guessed the full extent of the hatred out there, would be so worried, so disappointed, so devastated.

Strawgirl would be hurt for Maybe. She would feel her pain. Maybe didn't want Strawgirl to have to feel it. So she didn't tell her that some children at school held their noses when she walked by, that some stuck out a foot so that she'd trip up and fall over. She didn't tell Strawgirl that, since her father's death, she was always the last one to be picked when they were choosing a netball team or a dancing partner.

And then there were the really big bullies – those who bullied with money and power and letters from lawyers. Those who threatened and blackmailed and terrorized until they got their own way – who ripped out landscapes and flattened farms and trampled on ordinary lives. How could a creature ever understand them?

Maybe preferred to try and put it all behind her. She took Strawgirl to the wishing well and told her how you could throw a coin down there and make a wish and your wish would come true. Strawgirl threw a coin down, closing her eyes. Maybe didn't ask her what she wished for. They both respected the first law of the wish: silence.

16

Time for Eviction

As the eviction date loomed the brothers began to lose patience. 'They've had long enough,' Harold said, dipping his soldiers into a very runny egg.

'Absolutely,' Arnold said, a little nervously. He had a sharp nose for trouble and felt apprehensive.

'After breakfast, we'll pay them a visit,' Harold said, and slurped a large gulp of strong coffee.

They got into the black Mercedes and sped off, down through the winding country lanes of the Highlands, past the glorious hills and the dark mysterious lochs. 'It is breathtaking around here,' Arnold said.

'Right enough. Sniff the air!' Jimmy said, rolling down the window.

'I can't stand all these little winding roads. Why didn't they do like the Romans and make them straight?' Harold said irritably. 'They make me feel sick.' Jimmy laughed, throwing back his head. The window in the back was wide open; his hair blew about in the wind.

'I rather like the old Highlands.' Arnold coughed nervously.

'This twin of mine has always been a sentimental idiot,' Harold said.

Suddenly, a beautiful red deer appeared high on the hill beside them as they rounded a bend. It stared at them for a long time, a haughty stare, as if the deer knew it was superior to humans, as if it felt proud of its imperial blood.

'Get a load of that creature!' Jimmy said. 'Christ. These deer are not joking, are they? They know what they're about.'

'What *are* you talking about?' Harold said, looking at Jimmy as if he'd just gone mad.

'They belong here more than we do, that's what I'm talking about, you big dunce,' Jimmy said, looking backwards at the deer which was still standing there, proud and gloriously red on the slope of the steep hill.

They drove down the extremely bumpy farm track. Maybe watched them from the distance, eyeing the black car suspiciously. She shouted to her mum, 'We've got visitors!' But her mum didn't appear at the top of the stairs.

Then, two tall, identical men and a smaller man walked straight into the kitchen. (The door was always open, but that was not the point.)

'Excuse *me*!' Maybe said, outraged.

'You're excused!' Harold said, smiling pleasantly.

'I mean, *you* should excuse yourself!' Maybe said, icily. 'This is my farm!'

'It is *not* your farm. You run the farm, yes, but you don't own it. I own this farm,' Harold said quietly.

'What?'

'I think you heard,' Harold said, a harder note creeping into his chillingly quiet voice.

Jimmy stood looking around the kitchen. Something was cooking on the Aga. There was a big slab of cheese, sweating a little on a wooden board. Butter glowed in a butter dish on the table. A round fresh loaf of bread looked so inviting that Jimmy would have loved to cut himself a slice and put a hunk of that cheese on it. A big bowl of red apples and oranges blazed in the centre of the table. The place really did look like a home.

'I know you own it!' said Maybe. 'It still doesn't give you the right to just march in here.'

'Let's start again, shall we?' Arnold said, motioning to his brother and Jimmy to walk out of the kitchen. They followed him, looking nonplussed. Arnold knocked three times on the door. Maybe yanked it open, still obviously not happy. 'Now,' Arnold said, 'Can we talk to your mother?'

'No. She doesn't talk,' Maybe said, firmly. 'Talk to me.'

'Very well then. Look, we know this is a difficult time for you and for that we are truly sorry. But progress is progress, business is business, and we do need to have you vacate these premises so that we can get ahead with our plans.'

'We're not moving,' Maybe said. 'You can't do this. We have our rights. We've lived here all my life. My father lived here all his life. You can't suddenly chuck us out when it suits you, even if we are tenants. I've been reading up, and tenants have rights, you know.'

Harold was astonished. Who did this kid think she was?

'We're not going to stand here arguing with a child,' he said, his voice louder now, and angry. 'We're here to deliver your last warning. Either you move willingly or we will have you moved. Simple as that. Come on,' Harold said to Arnold and Jimmy.

Arnold placed the latest letter on the table next to the bowl of fruit. 'Give your mother this letter. It details our generous offer of compensation and gives her the dates for vacating the premises.'

'This is our home!' Maybe shouted. 'It is not "the premises".'

Jimmy sniffed awkwardly. To be honest, he felt sorry for the wee girl. He'd never been involved in moving somebody from his or her home before. It was a nasty business.

Harold leaned too close to Maybe's face and said, 'Make your mother understand. Be in no doubt. We are completely serious in our intentions. If you don't move willingly, we will move you. We are experts. Don't mess with experts.'

Maybe was incensed. She wanted to set the geese on them, but it would take more than that, much more than that. The tall twins and the smaller man left Maybe's kitchen. The small one left last and looked back at her, smiling a little apologetically.

Maybe felt her heart sink. 'Strawgirl?' she said.

Strawgirl came down from the ceiling where she had been lying watching everything, flat and inconspicuous. People rarely looked up at ceilings. 'Same men blond,' she said. 'Heads say, terrible time.'

Maybe stared at Strawgirl blankly. She didn't have a clue what her friend meant. Perhaps Strawgirl could read the future by looking at the tops of people's heads, their crowns, the way that some people can read hands or tea leaves or crystal balls or Greek coffee. Perhaps it was to do with the shape the hair made when it parted. What did Maybe know? She knew nothing.

There was a sick feeling of worry in Maybe's stomach. She loved her farm. She loved her cows, Birthday, Lipstick and Milkshake. She couldn't bear the thought of anything happening to them. It would make her lose her dad all over again.

'Maybe?' her mum called from upstairs. 'Who was that?'

Maybe climbed slowly up the stairs to her mum's bedroom. Irene was still in bed, her white, hard leg resting on several pillows. Strawgirl stood outside the room, waiting. 'It was the Barnes-Gutteridges. They've left another threatening letter.'

'Oh,' said Irene. 'Perhaps we should move. What's the point in fighting them? It will just use up our energy.'

Maybe stared at her mother in disbelief. Irene lay in bed, her hair a mess, her breakfast plate lying on top of the sheets, three empty mugs at the side of her bed. Wet tissues were strewn about the floor.

'What!' Maybe said. 'Mum! We can't give up. We can't let them win.' She wanted to shake her mother, to make her get up and wash, to make her bed, to make her tidy up after herself. Most of all, Maybe was desperate for her mother to show some interest, to care. It seemed she just didn't bother any more about anything – her farm, her daughter, her cows, their slaughter, anything.

'They say we've got to move in one month's time,' Maybe said, practically hyperventilating.

It was all too much. Her mother struggled with herself. The way she felt, they could drive a bulldozer through the whole farm. It was not the same place now that Jamie had gone.

'Dad would be livid,' Maybe said, enraged by her mother's response.

'He would, wouldn't he?' Irene said, nodding dreamily.

'Well?' Maybe said, hand on hip, waiting.

'I don't see how we can fight it, Maybe. I'm not well yet and we've no money to pay lawyers. Let me sleep on it.'

'That's all you do!' Maybe screamed at her. 'Sleep, sleep, sleep, sleep, sleep. Get up and *do* something!'

Irene rose listlessly from the bed, hobbled across the room on her crutches and combed her hair. It was a start – of sorts. The wardrobe door was open. Jamie's shirts still hung from the hangers: the checked shirts, the white shirts, the dark shirts, a row of his smart jackets and trousers. Irene wouldn't throw them out. They looked as if they were waiting for Jamie to come home. Every time Maybe caught sight of them, they upset her. She would give anything if her dad could just appear, dressed in that white shirt with those dark trousers and that tie, the tie she'd always hated. She'd never complain again about work on the farm. She would never tease him about his ties. If he could only walk miraculously out of the wardrobe and back into his life!

17

Autumn

When the seasons changed, Strawgirl seemed to change too. Her eyes were as bright and as pagan as conkers. Her straw hair flamed amber and gold. Her voice rustled like dried leaves skittered along by the wind. Maybe looked into Strawgirl's eyes and was surprised to see that they had changed to the colour of autumn fruits. It was as if Strawgirl too had her own harvest, a harvest of body and soul.

Maybe couldn't wait to see what Strawgirl would make of Hallowe'en or fireworks night in the village. She might hide in the barn, frightened of fireworks and bonfires, of Catherine wheels and bangers and rockets and crackling guys. For special occasions, Maybe might tie her tartan scarf round the sheaf of Strawgirl's straw throat.

It was a damp autumn night. Maybe looked out of her window and saw Strawgirl running across the fields through the gloaming, vanishing into the browns and reds and yellows and golds of the land. High above her, a kestrel trod air, searching for a mouse or a vole with its hard gold eyes. Autumn was like a hare staring up at the moon with gold coins for eyes. Autumn: the time when the sun crosses the equator as it proceeds southwards.

The leaves were orange and yellow and crunchy. They wept continually from the trees as though the land was bereaved. Strawgirl moved through the woods like their spirit, beautiful, sad, the last orange glow of evening light pouring through her hands into the dark shadows gathering on the ground. Soon winter would come to Wishing Well Farm. Soon all the trees would be stark and bare.

18

A Chance to Fly

It was past midnight now. There was a big full moon in the sky with a pale-orange light surrounding it. Strawgirl was in the barn, getting ready to go and wake Maybe up. There was a side to Strawgirl that Maybe had never seen. Strawgirl was part of nature and she was quick as a fox, vicious as an owl, jealous as an eagle. She spotted a mouse on the barn floor. She crept up on it, tense and excited. Her breathing was different. She pounced. The mouse screamed. Strawgirl skinned the mouse with her sharp straw fingers. She savoured the blood-raw flesh. Nature was tough, she thought to herself, tucking into the mouse's liver and then swallowing the intestines, kidneys and heart. She saved the tail for the end, sucking it up like spaghetti. Nature was tough, but tasty.

She wiped the blood from her fingers under the outside tap. The water was cold. She put her mouth under it and took a drink. She was fuelled up for the journey to Cull Castle – for whatever might await them. The night air had a sharp nip at the back of its long throat. The human girl would have to wrap up warm.

Strawgirl opened the kitchen door and climbed softly through the house till she reached Maybe's bedroom. 'Maybe,' she whispered quietly at first, then louder and more urgently. 'Maybe!' She pressed her face to Maybe's sleeping face. Maybe looked so beautiful asleep, it was a pity to wake her. 'Wake up, Maybe, wake up.' She shook her gently awake.

'What's happening?' Maybe asked, shocked and delighted.

'Cull Castle,' Strawgirl said.

'How are we going to get there?' Maybe asked as they slipped outside and into the dark night. 'I can't drive the tractor all that way. I'd get arrested if I drove the car, even though I *can* actually drive a car, you know.'

'Fly,' Strawgirl said. 'Fly night stars.'

Maybe tried to imagine it: flying up into the black night sky, up among the glittering stars – the Bear, Orion, the brightest light in the sky, Venus; the good moon as their guide.

'Trust me,' Strawgirl whispered.

Maybe was terrified. She wasn't one of those kids who had always wanted to fly, or who liked pretending they could fly – standing on steps and jumping off, arms akimbo. No, not Maybe. She didn't like heights if she was perfectly honest. Which meant life was quite tough in the Highlands. She had never in her eleven-year life been on an aeroplane, a helicopter, or anything with wings. She had once been offered a chance to go up into the sky in a hot-air balloon and she didn't take it, much to her father's disappointment. (It was a special birthday treat for her seventh birthday.) Once, at a carnival, she screamed herself sick on the big wheel and had never been back since.

Yet now here was the chance to save Wishing Well by climbing on Strawgirl's back and flying to Cull Castle where the Barnes-Gutteridge brothers lived. Could she take the chance? Was she up for it? Maybe! After another thirteen moments of hesitation, trembling, goose bumps and dizziness, Maybe jumped on to Strawgirl's back and they flew up and up and up into the big dark sky, the stars glittering and shining like the jewellery her mother used to wear. 'Do you think the stars taste of anything?' Maybe shouted into Strawgirl's ear.

'Peppermint,' Strawgirl roared back.

'Yes!' shouted Maybe. Actually, now she could sense the feeling of exhilaration coming in over a cloud. This was totally amazing. This was so fan-peppermint-tastic. What a thrill to see the roofs of farms and cottages, a few small blinking lights down below – to see the dark hooded tops of trees, to sniff the rain near where the rain was made. What a thrill to be out in the open night, on top of the world.

Maybe screamed in pleasure. This was just too good. But soon Strawgirl's outstretched arms brought them into the vicinity of Cull Castle. Even this high

107

up, the air above the castle tasted different: putrid. Maybe coughed. Down there, it was dense fog. Strawgirl's night eyes lit up the old turrets, the east wing, the west wing. It was time to land. Which window to fly in? They all looked shut. But there was one tiny window in the west wing that looked slightly open. They flew down, down, slowly, over the tops of the pine trees. The wind blew straight into their excited faces.

19

Inside Cull Castle

Sure enough, there was the small window, a fraction open. Strawgirl pushed it with her strong straw hands. It wouldn't budge. Maybe tried to push it too. It still refused to budge. They both pushed together – one, two, three. The window cracked open, and something crashed to the ground. They jumped down into the castle. It was a wedding photograph of Harold and Albert's parents; the father looked like an older version of the twins. The glass on the front was smashed, but the wooden frame was intact. They put it back on the window ledge. Luckily, nobody had woken up. The castle was quiet except for the noise of an ancient boiler, burbling away like somebody muttering and stuttering in their sleep.

They had landed on the top floor of the castle. Instinctively, Maybe felt they should head for the basement, the dark cellars, the dungeons. 'Secrets are usually kept underground,' she whispered to Strawgirl authoritatively. Secrets were rarely stored above, unless there was an attic. They walked quietly, swiftly, down one large set of stairs and down another, till they reached an old, spiral stone staircase. Their hearts were in their mouths. Maybe could barely breathe; even the normally calm Strawgirl looked perturbed, her straw flapping and trembling a little, her dark coal eyes darting from one end of the corridor to the other to check they were still alone.

Something moved at the end of the corridor. Maybe clutched at Strawgirl. 'What's that? Look!'

Strawgirl's eyes lit up a black cat in the distance. The cat's paws clawed, the outstretched talons picking and plucking at the carpet obsessively. They were lucky it was a cat, not a dog. The cat's noises were not likely to raise any human being from slumber. The cat sensed that Strawgirl was strange in some threatening way and sensibly walked in the opposite direction, her back high and rigid. When she was a little way down the corridor, she ran, streaking off into one of the rooms. Strawgirl overheard a voice say, 'What is it, Princess?'

'Quick, cat woke!' Strawgirl whispered urgently to Maybe. They rushed down the winding staircase as fast as they could manage. The steps were old and uneven, and extremely steep. Maybe lost her footing on one and twisted her ankle. But there was no time, no time to stand and rub at a swollen ankle. She had to continue, limping. 'Come on!' hissed Strawgirl. 'Hurry!'

A small, dark wooden door led down to the dungeons. The floor was slightly wet here and it smelled musty and damp. Maybe reached for a light switch then thought better of it. A light might attract unwanted attention. She turned to look at Strawgirl, and suddenly Strawgirl's eyes lit up and a yellow light flowed out of her straw head, illuminating the way forward. Some distance in front of them was a large oak trestle-table; it looked very old. On top of the table was a black folder labelled *The MacPherson File*.

Maybe opened the file. Inside were several letters, notes and pieces of paper. The first note, in big uneven letters cut out of a newspaper, read: *If you don't move by the end of the month something will happen to two of your cows*. The note wasn't signed.

The second note read: *If you don't move by the end of this week, kiss goodbye to four cows.*

The third note read: *If you don't move by Friday eight more of your cows will die.*

They were obviously blackmail letters. Behind them was a scrap of paper with the words *Malkie, Abattoir*, and a phone number. Underneath the phone number was the most chilling note of all: *SLAUGHTER DAYS – every second Friday of the month.*

In total and utter disbelief, Maybe read a hand-written document entitled:

Arnold – just to recap:
If the MacPhersons won't rehouse themselves and
their cattle, we will need to take matters into
our own hands. Legally, we can do nothing to
force them but we can prove we mean business
by stealing two of the cows and having them
slaughtered for starters. Have spoken with
Malkie who runs illegal abattoir. Cows will have
to be brought to him in the middle of the night.
It will work like this: we will bring the cows to
Cull in a horse trailer. We will then transfer them
to an unmarked, untraceable vehicle and take
them over the hills to the abattoir. Transporting
the cows shouldn't be difficult. Basically, it's a
matter of putting the halter on the beast and
dragging it along. We'll do this to the
MacPhersons until they cave in. – Harold

Maybe read it again. She thought of The Empress,
of Blossom, Bessie, Birthday, Madame Bovary. She
thought of Memphis Minnie, Sargasso Sea, Sleekit,
Lady Day and Lipstick. She thought of Lady Day's
big dark eyes, of the fine white chest of Tattie Scone,
of the wild, knowing stare of Wuthering Heights. It
was too much to contemplate. She had to prevent
this from happening. She had to save her cows from
mass extermination, from mass destruction. 'Oh,
Strawgirl!' she cried. She doubted that even

Strawgirl's powers were strong enough to defy evil like this.

'Bring!' Strawgirl said, pointing to the papers. Maybe nodded. 'Let's hope that they don't come down tomorrow. It says here that they plan to drive a massive bulldozer right through the heart of Wishing Well, ripping down the barns, the outbuildings and the farmhouse itself. The plan is to blooter the lot!' She let out a gasp as she came across her own name. There was a black line drawn through the name James MacPherson. It was the saddest sign Maybe had seen yet of her father's death, every bit as bad as the coffin behind the curtain that sickening day. Next to his name was her mother's: Irene Janet MacPherson. Then Molly Siobhan MacPherson. It referred to them as nuisances and pests and said they would have 'one hell of a fight'.

Maybe stuffed the papers in her pocket. She had no idea what she was going to do with them, but they were evidence. The men had no right to steal their cows, to intimidate them into doing what they wanted. That had to be illegal, didn't it? That had to be against the law.

Maybe followed Strawgirl quietly up the steep, dark stone staircase. But when they got to the top, they found the dungeon door closed and locked. There was a loud laugh from the other side. Then they heard a voice say, 'Thank God for cats. If it weren't for Princess, we wouldn't have known what the brats were up to.'

'How many of them are there? Did you see?' another voice asked.

'No, I just saw the MacPherson girl, but she's got to be with a friend. I heard her talking,' the man with the strong Glasgow accent said.

Then the second voice said, 'We can't keep them down there forever, you know. They'll starve.'

'Be quiet, you wimp!' the first voice said. 'One night down there will scare them nicely. Now, let's get back to sleep. I hate my sleep being interrupted. We'll think what to do with them in the morning. We could do them for breaking and entering. But we might be best not to involve the police. Let's get some kip, sleep on it. I'm done in. Actually, let's have a nightcap first. Let's have a malt for the road.' They heard the steps quicken and fade away into the distance.

Maybe was so petrified she couldn't shed a single tear, so frightened she could barely speak. In fact, she could barely breathe. Twice now in her life she had experienced the chill of terror, the icy slap of fear: the day her father had died and tonight, past midnight at Cull Castle.

It was a windy, disturbed night. The wind whistled through the castle's draughty corridors and rattled the dungeon door. Maybe thought it sounded like ghosts trying to get out. There was a scraping, scratching, scuttling noise in the corner. The old grandfather clock in the hall above struck one. The chime moaned for ages as if it was trapped in the clock. Maybe thought of her father trapped in his coffin. An owl outside hooted, a long, low sound, serious and solemn, as if it had just heard some very bad news.

20

Irene Alone

It was three in the morning. Irene MacPherson did not sleep too well these nights, despite what her daughter thought. Even with her plaster removed now, she still couldn't get comfortable. She was up and down, up and down. Scenes from the accident still flashed through her head. Jamie's face. She relived the moment over and over again. 'If onlys' visited and haunted her. If only they hadn't gone out that night. If only Jamie hadn't been distressed about those bullies. If only it hadn't been raining. If only, if only, if only.

Irene rose and went down to the kitchen to make a cup of tea. She stood by the kettle, waiting for it to boil. She put some milk in and sat in the arm-chair to drink her tea. The house was quiet, empty. She felt especially alone at night. There was no Jamie to snuggle up to. The space next to her in the bed was too large. She couldn't imagine ever having a proper, blissful, dreamy night's sleep again. Her sleep was the stuff of nightmares. She woke herself up calling out hoarsely, usually screaming Jamie's name.

Every night since Jamie died, Irene had got up in the middle of the night and made herself a cup of tea and sat in the kitchen by the warm Aga drinking it. Memories of Jamie mixed themselves up in her head. The day they first met at the dance hall in Aberdeen. Irene remembered saying to her pal Helen, 'Who is that drop-dead gorgeous black guy?' She remembered the feeling she had when she danced with Jamie for the first time. It was so good; Irene had felt like a wonderful dancer. She remembered the way he held her as they mooned around the dance floor, their bodies seeming to fit, to belong together already.

She remembered Jamie's eyes when Maybe was being born. The way he'd stared at her, saying, 'You're going to be all right. Breathe in. Breathe out. That's it. You're doing great. Push.' Jamie had been at her side throughout the whole birth. She couldn't have done it without him. She remembered how they'd both cried when Maybe was a few minutes old, lying across Irene's chest, tiny and wrinkled and new. 'She's ours,' Jamie had said, crying. 'I can't believe it. We've got a daughter.' Jamie had kissed Irene, then kissed the floury baby, her skin still covered with a thin film.

Irene usually finished her tea and went back to bed, to lie and stare at the strange cracks in the ceiling, like X-rays of fractures.

For some reason, tonight, she looked in on Maybe.

Later she wasn't certain what had made her do this – call it a mother's instinct, perhaps prompted by remembering Maybe's birth. Call it what you will, but Irene popped her head round Maybe's bedroom door, intending to go and kiss her while she slept.

She tiptoed across Maybe's bedroom to her bed. She pulled back the sheets – only to find pillows! Maybe was not there. She was not in her bed! Irene felt a rising panic reach straight up her throat and slide back down to her stomach. An acid taste in her mouth. Mouth dry. Her stomach burned. Palms sweated. Head went all hot. It was nearly four in the morning.

She dashed down the stairs and looked in the living room. It occurred to her that Maybe might be mad enough to go and sleep with the cows. She put on her wellington boots and ran quickly to the barn. The cows stared at her. They knew Irene and remembered her, although they hadn't seen her for some time. Maybe was not there.

Irene's mind couldn't make sense of anything. All sorts of dreadful thoughts rushed through her head at a terrifying speed. Perhaps her daughter had been kidnapped. Perhaps she would receive a ransom note. Perhaps she had run away, angry with her mother for not standing up to the Barnes-Gutteridges. Maybe the brothers had something to do with it! No, that was insane. Irene didn't stand there thinking any longer. She rushed into the house and picked up the phone.

It was the fastest she had moved since Jamie died. She dialled 999.

She thundered upstairs to put her clothes on. She would have to be ready. She shoved on a pair of jeans and an old navy-blue jumper. She stood, agitated, by the front window waiting to see the headlights of a police car coming down the dirt track.

21

Sizing Up the Joint

'Get up!' said Harold to Arnold. It was four in the morning. 'I can't sleep. We may as well use this opportunity to go and check that farm out again, seeing as we've got the girl and her meddling mates locked up in the dungeon.'

'What? It's the middle of the night!'

'Yes, precisely. It is the middle of the night. Get up, you lazy lump!'

In the grey hours before dawn, Jimmy and the brothers returned to Wishing Well Farm to draw up the final plans. They needed to decide on a running order for demolishing the buildings. Domino Supermarkets would not buy the land unless the MacPhersons were gone and the buildings down. If they didn't move quickly the potential deal would collapse. They needed to get the lie of the land and work out how long it would take them to steal the first two cows and transport them initially to Cull Castle, then on to the abattoir.

Harold was in charge of the 'architectural' plans.

In the kitchen, before they left for the farm, Harold held out a large, beautifully drawn plan of Wishing Well Farm and the land around it. 'This is the surrounding *environs*,' he said, pointing to the drawing. He said the word 'environs' as if he were French.

It annoyed Jimmy when Harold tried to remind him that he'd had a better education. Jimmy said the word back to Harold. *'On veer ons?'* It sounded like something fancy you could eat, like the French for snails. 'What the bloody hell is that, you posh swine?'

Harold exchanged a pitying look with Arnold. 'The surrounding area, my man. Now look here.' He held the large plan out wide. It stretched from Jimmy to Arnold. 'Hold an end – watch what you're doing!' he said, impatiently. 'Now, here is the main farm building. This is a little porch, I think. Here's the milking parlour. Here are the hay sheds . . . Here are the two barns; that's where the cows sleep. Apparently, the damn creatures only need four hours' sleep a night and have incredibly good hearing. Also, another tricky thing – they can smell you coming.'

'What? They'll smell us? You're kidding me,' Jimmy said. 'Away you go. I take a bath every day.'

'They can even smell sweet-smelling humans coming. Any stranger is identified by the cow's nose. Immediately! The cow isn't placid when she's threatened. No, the herd can turn wild and literally charge at you like an army.'

'Away you go,' Jimmy said. 'I dinny fancy this much.'

'I'm inclined to agree with Jimmy,' Arnold said.

'Let's get off now to the farm and check it out,' Harold said.

The men got their coats on and drove towards Wishing Well in the Mercedes.

'So how do we propose to get around this problem?' Jimmy continued the conversation in the car. It was still dark outside – not a thick darkness, but a thin, fragile darkness that the light would soon edge through. 'What are we going to do?' Jimmy asked, sitting in the back seat. 'I mean, a job's a job – it's no' worth getting trampled on by a hefty great herd of crazy coos.' Jimmy didn't tell the brothers that he had worked with cows before, that he was actually quite competent with them. He didn't like the idea of transporting the Wishing Well cows to an abattoir, and was hoping to put the brothers off, to scare them. As far as Jimmy was concerned, the twins were both, in different ways, total cowards.

'Well . . . I've talked about this with Malkie, the man from the abattoir, and he suggests sedating the beasts,' Harold said. 'He's even going to give us the medicine.'

'Why won't he do the job for us and take them himself?' Jimmy asked.

'He can't get involved in that way. His abattoir is too risky. The security checks on moving cattle are very tough. He says if we get the beasts to him, he'll pay us. He's even providing us with the second unmarked vehicle, which he uses for transporting illegal animals.'

'How are we going to get close enough to the coos to inject them, big man?' Jimmy said, while Arnold stood gaping, open-mouthed and horrified.

'Look, bro', we're selling our land, we're not qualified to sedate cows,' Arnold added.

'The Domino people want to move fast on building this supermarket. If we can have the MacPhersons out soon so that they can begin the development, they will pay the full price. If not, the deal could be called off. We need to scare them.'

'OK, we'll do it!' Jimmy and Arnold said simultaneously.

'The important thing is that we are all agreed: before we demolish the farm buildings marked A, B, C and D here on the map, we will have to move a couple of cows from the building marked D, to Cull. We will hire a horsebox trailer to transport them in. That should be manageable. We don't want to have to kill the whole herd. If we get rid of two, that should encourage them to sell the other cows themselves to another farmer. If not, we'll take more until they do. They'll never be able to prove it was us. Oh, and I've been reading up on how to inject cows.'

Harold parked the Mercedes at the end of the farm road; he didn't want to risk being seen. They started to walk down the dirt track towards the farm. 'It's no' going to be a doddle, this,' Jimmy said, puffing out the night air, pretending to smoke. Jimmy had given up smoking five years ago, but he liked a cold night when he could see his breath in front of him, when he could pretend he was exhaling the smoke of a big fat cigar.

'A what?' Arnold asked.

'A doddle. It's no' easy, in other words,' Jimmy said, tapping his finger to let the imaginary ash fall to the dust.

'I rather like that, don't you, bro'? A doddle.' Harold imitated Jimmy's Glasgow accent. 'A doddle. A wee doddle.'

Arnold barked a laugh. 'A doddle.'

'Shut yer geggies!' Jimmy said. 'If you can say "environs", I can say "doddle".'

Harold was about to say 'geggie' the way Jimmy said it, but thought better of it. Jimmy was a wee bit touchy; he had a chip on his shoulder. He had a whole fish supper on the other one.

'Right, men, we're agreed then. We will begin shifting two cows the day after tomorrow. Let's take a peek at them now.' Harold enjoyed being the leader. He was wasted here really; he could have been a general in Ancient Rome.

They walked on round the bend. They were just about to go further when they saw the twirling lights of a police car outside the farm door. 'What's going on?' Jimmy said.

'Damn!' Harold said, panic in his voice. 'They've discovered the girl is missing. We'd better get back to the castle. This whole situation could turn really

124

nasty. I thought that mother never got out of her bed. What's she doing up in the middle of the bloody night?'

'I don't know, but we'd better take a look at the cows another time,' Arnold said, and started to run at a nippy pace back to the parked car. Harold and Jimmy followed. Jimmy overtook Harold. Everything was a competition for Jimmy, even a run in the dark. He looked behind him; the twins were way back, out of breath. 'Those posh twins are no' as fit as me,' Jimmy thought to himself, pleased with his level of fitness, with his hard stomach, his six pack.

'We'll have to come back and size up the joint the morrow,' Jimmy said.

'That's it, Jimmy. Leave it to the morrow,' Harold said. 'Damnation! That's all we need, the police involved.'

'Are you taking the mickey?' Jimmy said suspiciously.

'No, I just love the way you talk, Jock.'

'You wouldn't know you two were Scottish, the way you talk, you know? That poncy boarding school has stripped you of a decent accent.'

'Steady on,' Arnold said. 'We're all supposed to be on the same side, aren't we?'

'Just joking,' Jimmy said and patted Harold's back. 'You don't get me, do you?'

'What do you mean "get you"?' Harold asked, patting Jimmy's back with even more gusto.

'That's what I mean. You don't understand me. I

might as well be an alien,' Jimmy said, shaking Harold off his back, irritably.

'Just a few barriers, I'm sure we'll get round them,' Arnold said, trying to keep the peace. All their lives his twin had had the unnerving ability to put people's backs up. Arnold didn't know how Harold managed it. Arnold himself just got along with chaps, but Harold got right under people's skin and scratched, and before long there were red rashes, big blotches.

'Let's drive back to Cull,' Arnold said, looking at Harold as if to say, 'And keep your mouth shut till Jimmy calms down.'

As they approached the black car, Jimmy said, 'Gie me the keys. I'll drive this time.' Harold flung him the keys and Jimmy pressed the little button that opened the central locking system. They climbed in, Jimmy turned on the ignition and put the car into first gear, pulling out slowly.

'Not too fast with the fuzz about,' Harold said. 'We need to get stopped by the police right now like we need a hole in the head.'

'Don't you think I know that?' Jimmy said defensively.

'I'm just saying,' Harold said.

'Ah, well. I'm just saying as well,' Jimmy said.

'Can I say something?' Arnold said.

Harold and Jimmy both looked at him expectantly. 'Shut up!'

'Nice brother that one,' Jimmy said to Harold.

'I know. Don't know where they got him from,' Harold said to Jimmy.

Arnold smiled. Well, at least they were both friendly again.

Jimmy drove the car safely back to the castle. They went through the wrought-iron gates, which opened automatically as they approached and then shut behind them. Harold was a big fan of security. It made him feel not only safe, but important. 'Want a brew?' Jimmy said, once inside the castle's kitchen.

'No time! We better go and sort those kids out,' Arnold said.

'Good idea,' Harold said.

Outside the castle, the big sky lightened; the sun was rising, slowly, shedding light on everything. Miles away, the sun made the red roof at Wishing Well Farm glow. A warm, yellow light, streaking and glinting over the brown and green fields, gave the impression that all was all right with the world. What did the sun know?

22

The Dungeon

It was cold down there at the bottom of the stone spiral staircase – cold and damp. Not a place for an eleven-year-old girl and her straw friend to hang out, long, long past midnight on a school night. Stuck there, in the dungeon dark, was like being trapped in the dark reaches of the identical men's minds. It was like being imprisoned by their cruel subconscious. There was no light to turn on. Maybe and Strawgirl tried every switch, but there were no light bulbs in the sockets. Maybe couldn't understand why Strawgirl's eyes weren't bright any more. Strawgirl explained that it was too late, or rather too early. Her eyes were only bright at night; the sun out there must be rising already. Strawgirl was like nature itself. You couldn't turn the sun on when it wasn't time for it to rise. You couldn't switch the moon off.

It was pitch-black and freezing cold down in the eerie dungeon, and there were no windows to escape from. Maybe felt something run across her foot. She was freaked out. She heard a terrible squeak and knew that rats were rattling about down there. The one living creature Maybe could not stand was the rat. A harmless country mouse, yes; a dormouse, a vole, a mole, she didn't mind. But rats were too big, with too-long tails. They carried all sorts of vile diseases – think plague – and they ran along sewers with a purposeful single-mindedness that was revolting. A pack of starving rats could eat them alive.

Something was dripping in the dungeon – a leaking tap, rain, it was difficult to tell. The steady drip, drip, drip noise was unnerving, like a ticking clock or a bomb. It made Maybe think something was telling them how long they had to live. Drip, drip, drip. Ten minutes; nine minutes and fifty-nine seconds; nine minutes and fifty-eight seconds; nine minutes and fifty-seven seconds. Drip. Drip. Drip.

'I can't see a thing,' Maybe said soberly. 'Just shapes. Sit close, Strawgirl. Don't move.'

Strawgirl told Maybe not to panic. 'Don't worry the dark.' She sat beside Maybe, stroking her hand. Although the straw scratched the back of Maybe's hand, it comforted her. She had grown used to the scratchy touch of Strawgirl and liked it. They sat like this for some time, Strawgirl and Maybe, holding hands.

After a bit Strawgirl said, 'Wall,' and pointed at the wall.

'What about the wall?' Maybe asked, perplexed.

Strawgirl made walking motions with her arms and pointed to the wall again.

'Walk through the wall?' Maybe exploded. 'Come off it, Strawgirl, that's impossible.'

'Who fly?'

'You.'

'And?'

'Me.'

'So?'

'No, but . . .'

'Trust me.'

'No! You are frightening me. I'm frightened enough already!' Maybe said, starting to cry.

It didn't seem possible that they could walk through the thick stone of the ancient castle, the stone that had been specifically built, hundreds of years ago, to keep out intruders. But then, a couple of hours ago it didn't seem possible that Maybe could fly through the open night air with the sizzling stars at her side and the streaky, dreamy clouds underneath her. There was no other choice. She had to save her cows from extermination and she had to act now. As soon as their plans were exposed to the outside world, the Barnes-Gutteridge twins would be finished.

'How do we do it?' Maybe said bravely, her mind resolved.

'Use mind,' Strawgirl said.

'What?' Maybe asked. Strawgirl pointed to her own head, then to Maybe's, then back to her own.

'Do you mean like telepathic communication?' Maybe asked, excited.

'Yes,' Strawgirl said, nodding seriously.

'Do you mean like identical twins? I've heard they can sometimes communicate like that even if they are miles apart.'

'Yes,' Strawgirl said again. 'Come.'

'Aiiii! I've had that with my mum sometimes. She calls it "being on the same wavelength".'

'Wavelength – good.'

Maybe looked down, unspeakably sad for a moment.

What?' Strawgirl asked gently.

'My mum and me aren't on the same wavelength any more. Not since my dad died. We're just not the same.'

'Don't worry. Come back.'

'Do you think so? Really? We'll get it back?'

'Course,' Strawgirl said. 'Course.'

Maybe smiled. She loved the idea of being close to her mum again.

'No time,' Strawgirl said, urgently. 'Quick. Close eyes. Trust.'

Maybe nodded in the darkness of the dungeon. This would have been very exciting if she wasn't trapped in a castle with the thought of her cows' imminent death.

'Calm, be calm,' Strawgirl said. 'Heavy, be heavy. Feet, neck, heavy. Limbs, feet, heavy. Arms, heavy. Hips, heavy. Back, heavy. Sink, sink, down. Now. Sleepy. Safe. Sleep. Float. Good. Float. Sleep, sleep, sleep.'

Maybe had never heard Strawgirl say so much.

She wished she could wake up to tell her that, but something was pulling Maybe down into slumber. She yawned. She couldn't help herself, she was falling asleep.

Maybe was unusually receptive to hypnosis. Some people were too uptight to respond like this, both children and adults. Strawgirl was proud of Maybe. She had just known that Maybe MacPherson would take to hypnosis, and that Maybe would have a wide-open mind. When Maybe's mind was completely open, Strawgirl could use her powers to pull them both through the wall.

'Now, open eyes.' Maybe opened her eyes. She was still hypnotized. 'Hand.' Maybe placed her hand in Strawgirl's.

'Body light, feel how light. Wall, now.'

Maybe and Strawgirl stood side by side, holding hands. They stepped towards the wall. 'Deep breath,' Strawgirl said. 'Now! Go!'

Maybe had a strange sensation of walking through another time period, of being way back in history. The sound of her breath was loud, as if she were inside herself blowing out, like someone in an oxygen tent. She smelled the bad odour of illness, of the Black Death, the plague, then the dreadful smell of fire, of burning flesh. Her body felt hot, then cold, then again hot.

She passed a leper who was wearing a coin amulet for luck. She hurried past people suffering from scrofula, with ghastly swollen necks. She clutched

Strawgirl's hand. She heard people crying out in pain. She passed an apothecary who was also a barber, shaving the back of a man's head. A woman was screaming as she gave birth. Maybe was as hot as a furnace. A fire roared and blazed in a fireplace. Behind a newborn baby, a dog gnawed on a bone. A rat ran past covered in fleas. She walked on till she came to the seventeenth century. A woman's forehead was covered in blemishes, near the roots of her hair – ugly red blotches. A man blinded from smallpox babbled and gabbled nonsense phrases. A small girl with a hole in her neck passed her. Maybe was petrified. She gripped Strawgirl's hand. The wall filled with the noise of children coughing, a great deep whoop of a cough that sounded like a terrible struggle for breath.

A young man with scurvy drifted by; he had rubbed the flowers of brimstone, sulphur, on his chest. She noticed a baby, no more than three months old, with two leeches on its foot, sucking its blood. Suddenly, she came upon a spa, a holy well full of good minerals. Sick people sat, sampling the healing water, fully clothed.

She continued on until she came to the middle of the eighteenth century. She heard the cries of the Highlanders in the Clearances. She heard the sound of sheep bleating, of the wild mountain wind. She saw cottages on fire, the roofs and the rafters lit up in one red blaze.

She passed through an entire outbreak of cholera.

Hundreds of people were squatting down with severe diarrhoea, vomiting on the ground. They looked weak, sleepy. The smell was revolting. Maybe covered her face, resisting the urge to vomit herself. A taste of bitter herbs filled her mouth. Maybe's forehead was hot and clammy. She felt dizzy. She didn't think she could take any more.

And then they were out. All of a sudden they were in the grounds of Cull Castle. Daylight shocked them. They stood blinking in disbelief. Maybe staggered about, trying to get her balance. The ground beneath her sank and came back. The terrible visions inside the wall had disappeared like ghosts; the wraith-like figures had returned to the past.

'Oh no, oh no, oh no. I don't believe we just did that,' Maybe said.

'Quick! Down!' Strawgirl said. 'Crawl.' They crawled along the castle grounds until they came to a square field. Maybe wanted to dance and sing and holler, but Strawgirl whispered fiercely, 'Not safe.'

They crawled through the tall pine trees, the flaky forest floor. The early morning light sprinkled down on them like confetti. Little chinks lit their way; a lemon path of light. Maybe's stomach was rumbling, she was so hungry. Strawgirl was also famished, but secretive. She didn't want Maybe to see her skin a mouse and eat it. There would be time for the raw grub later. They needed to get back to the farm.

It was still early in the morning. Maybe hoped against hope that her mum had not woken up and discovered her missing. Mind you, she slept so much these days it was unlikely Irene would know anything. All Maybe needed to do was creep back in through her bedroom window.

They found a bit of a hill. Strawgirl said, 'Up, up, up!'

They stood on the top of the small hillock with their arms outstretched. 'Lift!' Strawgirl shouted. 'Concentrate. Lift!' And they rose, the pair of them together like two beautiful birds with open wings. There was nothing like it. Maybe had come a long way from the girl who was afraid of flying. Into the sky they soared, flying separately through the wistful clouds, which looked like whisked egg whites. Maybe's eyes shone in the morning light.

She was as high as a folk song; pure notes flew out of her heart through the fresh autumn air. She passed over her familiar hills and mountains, browns and oranges. She reached out to stroke them – the land, her beloved land. It seemed as if it knew her. The top of the hill curled its shoulder pleasantly. She rubbed under the long jaw of Ben Kildonan.

'The mountain is moving!' she shrieked to Strawgirl.

'No!' Strawgirl shouted back. But Maybe didn't believe her. If she could fly and walk through walls, then surely a mountain could move a little. She remembered a song she'd been learning in school. She sang as she flew:

'At last into the mountains I'm returning, I'm
    returning,
Oh, mountains of my childhood, I'm returning to
    thee.'

Strawgirl looked behind her and laughed. She had
never seen Maybe this happy.

The flashing lights of the police car were there, next
to the farmhouse. They reminded Maybe of the night
her father had died, when she had seen the screaming,
rotating light flash through the window. Seeing the
police, just setting eyes on their uniform, was enough
to make her think she was in trouble.

She couldn't come in through the window because
they wouldn't believe she could fly, and she didn't
want them to disbelieve a single word she said. She
landed next to the field where her cows were making
a lot of noise. When they recognized Maybe, they
quietened down.

Annie and Fred had just finished the early morning
milking and were leading the cows back to the
pasture. Annie turned round to see Maybe walking
towards her.

'Maybe!' Annie shouted.

'When you didn't come, we decided to start the
milking anyway,' Fred said. 'Mind you, they missed
you. Where have you been? Your mother's worried
sick. The police are here!'

Annie flapped her arms. 'Quick! Rush and tell your

mum you are all right. Where have you been? No, don't tell me. Tell them.' She propelled Maybe around and marched her forward.

A policeman was in the kitchen. He had been questioning Irene MacPherson for the past hour.

'Mum!' Maybe shouted. Irene turned around; her face was one big O of surprise like an open cave. Her eyes were so wide, her eyeballs could have fallen out and rolled on the floor.

'Maybe! Where have you been?' Irene clutched at her. Maybe sobbed into her mother's chest. The entire ordeal – the dark of the dungeon and the terror of the wall – sank in as soon as she saw her mum.

One look at her mother – her red hair, her green eyes – was enough to make Maybe feel safe. She rested her head on her mother's chest as Strawgirl slipped unnoticed on to an open beam. Strawgirl had nobody to hold her, to tell her she was home safe.

23

What a Cock and Bull Story

Sergeant Pawlinski rubbed his black hair under his police hat. 'Let's run through this again, shall we? You're telling me that you got these papers at Cull Castle tonight?'

'Yes,' Maybe said, a little irritably. This was the fourth run-through. He didn't believe her. She knew he didn't believe her. He was wasting precious time; he should be asking his questions at the castle.

'How did you get all the way over to Cull Castle from here? It is a good eleven miles. You couldn't have walked.'

Maybe knew better than to say, 'I flew,' so she said, 'I ran.'

'That's an impossibility.'

Irene MacPherson intervened. 'Molly, you'll have to tell the Sergeant the truth.'

How could she tell the truth? How could she tell them about Strawgirl for starters, about flying through the air for seconds, about walking through walls for thirds? It was absurd. She knew they wouldn't buy any of it.

'OK, I did something very dangerous, so don't be angry,' she told her mother. 'I hitched a lift.'

'What? There and back in the dead of night? I don't think so,' the Sergeant scoffed.

'I did. Look, go to the Castle and look down in the dungeon. I can describe it to you exactly. How could I describe it to you if I hadn't been there? Where do you think I got this file from?'

The Sergeant looked at the papers. 'These blackmail letters could have been made by anybody. A child could have made them.' He looked straight at Maybe.

'Me?' Maybe said, outraged. 'You don't think I'd write notes to myself about my own cows!'

The Sergeant looked as if that was exactly what he thought. He gave her a pitying look. 'How long is it since your dad died?'

'Mum!' Maybe said. 'It's those brothers you need to be questioning, not me. Tell him! Tell him I couldn't dream up this sort of stuff.'

Irene spoke gently. 'Maybe, go up to your room and get ready for school, and I'll talk to this policeman.'

'You have to believe me,' she screamed, 'or our cows will be killed! Please!' But Irene's face was sad and serious. Maybe left the room, reluctantly.

'Molly would never think up something like this,' Irene told the Sergeant. 'She is simply not capable of it. There has to be some other explanation.' Sergeant Pawlinksi looked dubious.

Irene thought of Maybe over the last few weeks – how passionately she wanted to stay on at Wishing Well. 'Perhaps Molly is tired and stressed, but if you are asking me whether she could do this,' Irene pointed at all the blackmail letters and the documents, 'I'd say no. Definitely not.'

'I hope you won't take this the wrong way,' Sergeant Pawlinksi said, 'but most of the parents we talk to don't think their children are capable of the crimes they commit.'

'I know my daughter!' Irene said indignantly.

'You'd be surprised. They all say that,' the Sergeant said. 'Look if it reassures you, I'll take a trip up to Cull Castle. I'd like to check out those Barnes-Gutteridges, anyway. I doubt they're involved in anything illegal, but I'll go and have a look if you like.'

'Yes, that might be a good idea,' Irene said, yawning. The whole episode was tiring her out. Perhaps Maybe *had* written the notes. What did she know? She'd hardly talked to her daughter properly for weeks. Irene felt a pang of guilt.

'She's been working herself silly, Molly has. She milks the cows twice a day. She practically runs this farm on her own.'

'Perhaps she needs a rest then. I'd suggest plenty of sleep. I think she's showing signs of mental disturbance. Your husband's death might have had quite a serious psychological effect on her. Young children can have nervous breakdowns, apparently,' said Pawlinski. 'Not just adults. Watch her carefully.'

'I don't like what you are implying,' Irene said, frowning. 'I will personally get to the bottom of this. There will be an explanation. Molly is *not* mentally disturbed. She's been keeping me going. She's been holding the fort.'

'Perhaps it's all been too much for her?' Pawlinski suggested mildly.

'No, it hasn't! Now, if you'll excuse me, Sergeant, I'll keep you posted.' Irene held the door open and Pawlinski walked through. He felt a bit rattled. He was just trying to help.

What other explanation could there be? Perhaps he should pay a visit to Cull Castle just to be sure? He decided that was exactly what he would do. It couldn't do any harm. Of course, he thought to himself, the wee girl was bonkers, but still, it wouldn't hurt to have a look.

Irene climbed the stairs to Maybe's room. She heard her talking and opened the door. 'Maybe? Who was that you were talking to?'

Strawgirl was up on the ceiling again. She had floated up there and was lying in the far right corner. 'Nobody. I wasn't talking,' Maybe said hastily.

'Oh.' Irene was confused. She had definitely heard Maybe talking. Perhaps Pawlinski was right. There was a distinct possibility that her daughter was going crazy.

'I think you'd better miss school today and have a

rest,' Irene said. 'I'll look after you. You can have a nice cup of hot chocolate and we can watch a movie . . .'

Maybe couldn't believe her ears. She rushed to her mum and put her arms round her. Strawgirl peered down from the ceiling. Maybe wondered if Strawgirl would like to have a mum to snuggle up to on the couch so they could watch a movie together, eat chocolate biscuits, for a treat, and drink hot chocolate. There was nothing she could do to help Strawgirl if she did want a mum. It didn't seem right: Strawgirl put herself out for Maybe all the time, but Maybe couldn't do anything for Strawgirl. Perhaps Strawgirl didn't want a mum anyway, Maybe thought. Maybe she does, maybe she doesn't.

Strawgirl flew outside into the rain. She lay down in the hay shed on top of a pile of bales and listened to the noise of the rain on the corrugated iron roof. Exhausted, she curled up on the straw and fell asleep. In the house, Maybe curled up with her mum on the sofa and watched *Grease* for about the hundredth time. She liked watching John Travolta dance, swinging those hips in tight jeans.

24

Dad

In her mind, Maybe had her dad's hands as he folded the wings of a paper bird. Maybe could still look at herself and see her father, close as she was to her mother. She could still picture him vividly in her mind: how he looked with his white shaving-cream beard in the mornings. She could still hear his snort of a laugh, and smell the warm smell of the farm in his checked shirts, mixed with his favourite aftershave. She could still see the flash of his gold tooth when he laughed and laughed.

In her ears, she heard his whistle when he came into the house – three low, a high, then a low. She could hear the Ibo lullaby he sang when she was ill:

Desse! Adeli! Lovely brown girl!
Come into the sun! Let it shine on you.
Your skin shines bright like the River Nile,
Your skin is smooth like an antelope's,
Carved like a wooden jewel box.
When you wear golden ornaments

You are like the Queen of Nubia,
Oh, lovely girl of golden brown!
Your babies will be numerous . . .

Maybe's legs were like her father's legs, long and thin. Her hair was like her father's hair, only her curls were not so tight. Her nose was wide like her father's nose, and when she was angry her nostrils flared like his did. Her tongue was like her father's tongue, thick and pink and speckled like an egg. Her eyes were as dark brown as her father's eyes, deep, rich brown, the colour of the moist earth. She had his small ears. She had his feet – long-toed, arched high, smelly. She even had his flashing white, broad teeth. How could she forget her father when so much of herself reminded her of him?

Her mother held her close. 'You remind me of him,' she said, hugging Maybe tighter as if she had heard her thoughts. 'When you smile,' Irene said softly, 'you are his exact double. It is quite uncanny. Really quite uncanny.'

Maybe smiled to herself and remembered Strawgirl telling her the wavelength would come back.

25

The PDA Comes for the Cows

Harold had checked that he had enough sedative to knock out the cows. In fact, he had enough of the medicine to put an entire herd to sleep. He'd picked up all the stuff they would need from Malkie, who had assured him that it was plenty for this hit and the next one and even the one after that. He had a big plastic bag containing sixteen large sterilized needles. He had three pairs of plastic gloves. One needle already loaded with sedative stuck out of his black raincoat pocket in a small plastic bag. Although it was not raining tonight, he had advised the other two to wear raincoats like him. That way, any splashes of cow urine, or worse, cow dung, could be washed off. He was nervous, but excited. Cruelty always has a bit of a buzz about it.

Boarding school had taught Harold all about callousness and malice. There, he had played constant pranks on the uninitiated, on the new boy, the weak boy, the boy with glasses, or the boy with bad acne. It had started off innocently enough. He once took a new boy's duvet and hid it in the freezer in the kitchen. It wasn't found for some time and when it was the feathers had frozen. That gave his whole dorm a good laugh and they picked Harold as Leader of the Tricks. By the time he was fifteen, he was dealing in more serious scams. He could send viruses to computer systems; he could hack into somebody else's files; he could do card fraud and cash fraud. Once, he even forged a passport and travelled under an assumed name, just for the fun of it, just to see if he could. He never, ever got caught, not even at school, because he was one step ahead of the game, and was good at being polite, innocent and obsequious. Most teachers didn't like him, he had no genuine charisma, but they couldn't point to why. He was always the first to say, 'Thank you,' but there was something smarmy and irritating about Harold that they just couldn't trust. 'Can't put my finger on it, but there's something unpleasant about that Harold Barnes-Gutteridge,' one master would say to another. 'He never comes clean. It's as if he is always hiding something, but one never knows what it is.'

'And he's got that nervy twin of his right under his thumb,' another master would say. But they could never prove anything, pin anything on him. Harold covered his tracks and always managed to blame somebody else.

The brothers and Jimmy climbed into the horsebox they had acquired specially for this job. It would surely frighten the girl into action, stealing two of her precious cows. The MacPhersons would soon notice the animals were missing, but what was there to link their disappearance with Cull Castle except the nonsense uttered by an eleven-year-old girl?

'Now, men, we must be exceedingly careful,' Harold told Arnold and Jimmy.

'Aye, nae bother,' Jimmy said. 'I'll keep my eyes peeled.'

'Because the police paid us a visit yesterday.'

'Really?' Jimmy said. It was the first he had heard of it. 'It must have been when I was out getting the shopping.'

'That girl stole some of our papers. I told the stupid Sergeant I'd never seen them before. But she's cleverer than we thought. I mean, how did she escape from the dungeon? The door was still locked and there are no windows down there. It's unsettling to say the least,' Harold said.

'I couldna believe my eyes that night when we opened the door and there was no girl,' Jimmy said, laughing with some pleasure.

'It wasn't funny,' Harold said.

'But what is she anyway? Some kind o' Houdini, eh? You've got to hand it to the lassie. Escaping from a dungeon is no bad doing. What did you say then to the fuzz?'

'I managed to bluff my way through things, deny all knowledge. But I'm not pleased. I'm really not pleased. I had to use every inch of my charm.'

'What charm?' Jimmy said. 'I've no' seen any charm. You aren't even polite to me.'

'Yes, well, this was a policeman. I was polite to him all right. Offered him a "wee dram". He didn't take it because he was on duty, but he was charmed. He didn't suspect a thing. The policeman thought the girl had had a nervous breakdown.'

'That's no' right,' Jimmy said, frowning. 'I hate it if anybody accuses me of being mad.'

'I don't suppose *that* happens very often,' Harold said with a faint hint of sarcasm in his voice.

Jimmy, luckily for Harold, because this was not the night to have arguments, didn't notice. 'Right enough,' he said, reasonably pleased. Jimmy suddenly had a thought. 'If those police have seen the notes, they'll know it is us when the cows disappear for real.'

'No, they won't. They don't trust the girl and her mother. They trust us.'

'But *they* will know – Molly and her mum will know it is us, now that you've been so stupid as to show your hand.'

'I didn't know the girl was going to come snooping here. Anyway, it's good if they know it is us. It's better really, then we can show them we mean business. Think about it. What can they do?'

Arnold was fidgety. He had never been comfortable with cats or dogs, let alone cows. All animals, from the very small to the very large, alarmed him. If he were left alone with a rabbit, he would feel uneasy;

he wasn't fond of their twitching noses. Even his twin's cat made Arnold edgy, the way she could walk with her back arched. Very creepy. People who kept snakes and lizards or other reptiles as pets were beyond the pale as far as Arnold was concerned. He was frightened of the high nervous energy of horses, but cows were the worst of the lot. He had never been fond of the way that cows stare, stare right through you, as if they knew every damn thing about you. Nor, if he was honest, had he ever liked the way they chew for ages and ages, their mouths lazily munching from side to side. Or the way every cow seemed to have heard the news about the weather; the way they all lay down instinctively when they suspected rain. They were spooky. Even the thought of the money from the Domino deal wasn't enough to galvanize him into action.

'Are you . . . are you sure this will work, bro'?' he asked Harold testily.

Harold knew his twin very well. All the signs were there. The red blotches on his face. The breathy voice. The shaking hands, never still for a minute. The left eye twitch. He was disgusted with his twin. Why could he not rely on him when he needed him?

'I hope you're not getting yourself in a state,' Harold warned Arnold. His voice had all the authority of someone six minutes older.

'No, I'm not in a state,' Arnold said quickly, out of breath.

'Good. Because we can't do "states" tonight. We

are doing "cows" tonight. Got it? And you have got to be strong. You can't let us down. Your job is the easiest. You have got to help get the cow into the trailer. I am the one who has to do the injecting with the help of Jimmy. I will drive, so there's really no problem. Now, pull yourself together!'

Jimmy eyed Arnold quickly. These twins were very strange men, he thought – one weak, one strong, like Jekyll and Hyde. Weird though, because they looked identical – so much so that at first Jimmy had trouble telling them apart. But as soon as he got to know their personalities, it was easy. Harold's blue eyes were colder and meaner; his nose was that little bit sharper. Arnold had watery eyes. But they were more or less the same height and build, and they had the same colour hair. They were even, damn them, quite handsome big blokes.

Jimmy was not handsome. Douggie Parker had broken his nose when he was eight and it had never mended. He still had the look about him of somebody in a poor boy's boxing match. He looked as if his sense of smell had been twisted to one side, and his eyes were sunk too far into his head. When he was younger, he used to wish he had a very brave friend who could have reached in and pulled his eye sockets a half-inch further forward. Then he would have felt the equal of anybody else. Jimmy's skin was pitted like the holes and crevices in the moon. Since boyhood, Jimmy had had the sensation that his looks were one big disadvantage. They affected his confidence. But it wasn't looks that counted; it was what you were like underneath. Then he thought, 'Why am I doing this? What kinda man am I to steal coos in the dead of night?' He had the thought, then he considered the money. 'Och, everybody has to earn a living somehow,' he said to himself.

Jimmy couldn't wait to finish this job though. He was going to use the money to buy his mother a modern electric wheelchair. At the moment, she was still using one of those old-fashioned ones and needed somebody to push her everywhere. Jimmy didn't like what he was doing, but he was desperate to earn the money. This was the weirdest job he had ever had. He wished he could press fast-forward to the first night after the job was done, when he would be sitting in his flat in Glasgow, a pint of beer in his hand and his feet up. Jimmy didn't intend staying on in the Highlands with the twins. He was homesick. He wanted to go back to Glasgow. He imagined the telly on and his fist inside a big bumper bag of smoky-bacon crisps.

26

Late at Night

Harold drove the trailer the eleven miles from Cull Castle to Wishing Well Farm, down the side of Loch Clash, through Badcall, Inshegra and Achriesgill, up the road towards Balnakeil Bay and finally to Grumbeg. The cows stood outside in their pasture (because it wasn't yet winter), already aware that something was wrong. They were not lying down. Cows have an alert sense of danger. Their hearing is as good as a dog's; their large earflaps can turn independently to help them work out where a sound is coming from.

Cows are prey animals. Strangers are potential predators. Like most prey animals, a cow's eyes are placed at the side of her head, so that her eyesight is perfect for panoramic vision. Like a camera, she can take a wide picture. That broad peripheral vision, those eyes at the side of her head, can sense the approach of a predator literally out of the corner of her eye.

Maybe and Irene were exhausted from the drama

of the last couple of days – not just days, but weeks of grief and worry. Despite Maybe's anxiety about her cows, she couldn't help falling off to sleep. Perhaps it was all nonsense. Perhaps the brothers' plans were just a bad-taste joke. Perhaps that was how the Barnes-Gutteridges got their thrills, by writing horrific plans of slaughter. That was it – just bad thoughts written down. Maybe convinced herself everything would work out as she fell asleep to dream of her dad, her dad and herself, running up and down the fields of barley. In her dream she was singing: *'Corn rigs and barley rigs, corn rigs and barley, oh.'*

Luckily, Strawgirl was not exhausted. She needed only three hours' sleep a night and she didn't usually bother trying to get that sleep until two in the morning. Tonight, she was out in the fields hunting for something to eat when she heard the sound of a strange vehicle.

Harold drove the horsebox down the bumpy dirt track. The men bounced up and down in it. The moon was watching. The sky was clear and the stars were astonishingly bright. Starlight sprayed the fields like a water sprinkler. It was a bitterly cold night, but good and dry. They were lucky it had not rained, that the sky was as clear tonight as it had ever been in all its billions of years.

The farmhouse was in total darkness; not a single

light shone through any of the windows. 'It looks like everybody is asleep,' Arnold observed.

'Yes, how innocent a house looks in darkness, so trusting,' Harold said, relishing the moment.

Jimmy looked at him quizzically. 'I wish we were asleep too,' he said. 'I'm no' looking forward to this, either.'

'That's not the way to talk. Good grief, do you think men in wartime looked forward to battle? No, they didn't. But they put their best foot forward,' Harold said sternly.

'But this is cattle, not battle,' said Jimmy and laughed at his own wee joke.

Arnold laughed too, loudly, his big bark of a laugh.

'Quiet!' Harold whispered viciously. 'Quiet!'

They got out of the trailer, where they had been sitting in a row of three, and jumped down. Though they knew the farm from the surveyor's plans, and they'd been there before, it still took a while before they got their bearings. 'If this is the farmhouse,' Jimmy said, pointing to his left, 'and that is the dairy,' he said, pointing to the building straight ahead and to the right, 'then that building next to it is the barn where they should be in their baw-baws, dreaming coo dreams.'

'Well done, James' Harold said. He had taken to calling Jimmy 'James', not Jock or Jimmy, to show the man the respect he deserved. Say what you would about the coarse Glasgow accent, the man was a hard-worker and no shirker. Once you got around the accent and actually understood what he was saying, you discovered that he was really quite intelligent.

Maybe was lying in her bed fast asleep, dreaming. She was too far into her deep sleep to hear Strawgirl rapping at her window, and much too deep in her dreams to hear Strawgirl whispering urgently, 'Maybe. Wake up! Wake up, Maybe!'

'Can't we get the trailer a bit nearer to the barn?' Jimmy said. 'We don't want to have too far to walk them.'

'Good thinking!' Harold said. 'You two go to the barn and I will meet you there,' he said, getting back into the trailer.

A couple of minutes later, Harold observed that Jimmy and Arnold were gesticulating madly to him, their hands out open, as if to say, 'Nothing doing.' He jumped down. 'What's the problem?'

'They're no' there, that's the problem,' said Jimmy.

Arnold was thinking they had been offered deliverance. 'Oh well bro', nothing we can do. We'll just have to leave it for tonight.'

'Don't be stupid!' Harold said irritably, thinking fast on his feet. 'Of course! It's still quite mild for September. They will be in the fields.' He shone his powerful flash lamp over the fields to their left. And there, sure enough, were sixty-four cows eyeing them suspiciously. 'Damn it all!' he said. 'Well, we'll just need to take them from the fields. How stupid of me! Stupid, stupid, stupid.'

The cows were agitated; they shuffled about in the field from hoof to hoof. They could smell the strangers approaching. They could tell they were a potential threat because their smell was unfamiliar and they didn't recognize their body stance. It was impossible to settle on the pasture. The cows were up, their big ears flapping, listening to the sound of the strange men approaching.

'Wait a minute,' Arnold said. 'How are we going to lead them from that field to the trailer?'

Harold climbed back into the horsebox to get his electric cattle prod and a long rope. 'With the help of this friend,' he said, brandishing the metal prod in the air. He switched it on and touched his twin with it to see if it was working. It sizzled on Arnold's forearm so that he jumped back.

'Don't mess around with that thing!' he shouted.

The cows bunched together as soon as they saw the men approaching. If the men stayed a safe distance away, the cows would remain grouped together like this in their herd. They needed enough space to feel safe from strangers, but the last thing Harold wanted to give these cows tonight was space. He walked straight up to them, crossing the line of their flight space. Harold knew nothing of flight space – the distance a cow needs to keep between herself and an intruder.

As the three of them walked towards the cows, the

animals scattered, running in different directions in the dark night. If they had been herding them, the men would have completely lost control. But it suited Harold that they were not a united, glaring, threatening bunch any more. He could now go after individual cows. One trembled next to the drystone wall. 'Hamburger! Steak Diane! Beef Stroganoff!' Harold whispered menacingly.

27

Jimmy's Expertise

'Which two shall we pick first?' Jimmy asked, looking at the cows that were scattered all over the pasture.

'Those two,' Harold said, pointing at the quivering cows nearest to them.

'We must walk slowly. Don't run. Don't make any sudden movements. We must be calm at all costs,' Jimmy said. 'If you chase a coo, it sees it as a predatory act.' Harold looked at him, clearly impressed. James seemed more articulate all of a sudden.

Maybe turned in her sleep to face her bedroom wall. Strawgirl tapped the window. Time was running out. There was the sound of the wind rustling through the trees, whistling and whispering into the dark. The trees shook, their long arms swaying and swishing up into the night sky. An owl hooted a note of grief in the distance.

'Did you hear that?' Arnold said to Harold. 'That

sounded like a barn owl. Look! There are bats up there. I hope they don't swoop down on us.'

'I didn't see anything,' Jimmy said, privately thinking that the second-born twin was losing it altogether.

'Nor I,' Harold said, looking at his twin scornfully. They walked slowly towards Little Pink and Lipstick.

The darkness didn't stop the cows' big eyes taking in the strangers. They swivelled their heads around and stamped their hooves. Their tails swung round and round like lassoos. They started to make a lot of noise – deep, harrowing moans, like the sounds of long, low notes on bagpipes.

Arnold was petrified. 'I want to turn back,' he said. 'Forget the money.'

'Look. We are here now. We are doing this. Be calm,' his twin ordered.

They walked slowly towards Little Pink and Lipstick. Even Harold was not feeling very brave. They approached Little Pink and prodded her in her bottom. She ran at them. They ran behind her and prodded her some more. She charged away to the back of the herd. So they tried Lipstick. Who said cows were docile? Lipstick kicked Arnold in the shins. She kicked sideways and backwards, in one powerful *thwack*. It practically cracked Arnold's tibia. 'Ouch!' he shouted, making the alarmed cows run further. 'That hurt.' He bent down to rub his leg. 'Damn. I think the bone's chipped.'

'Never mind that,' Harold said. 'Grow up!'

Third cow lucky maybe? They approached Milk-shake from the front, making the fatal mistake of getting too close to her head. She butted Harold, and he fell back on to the grass. Then she made a dash for the back of the field. Harold picked himself up and wiped down his raincoat with his hands. 'Just as well I wore this,' he said, attempting a brave laugh. But Jimmy eyed him closely. It was the first time he had seen the guy truly shaken up.

Maybe turned in her bed and yawned. 'What was that at the window?'

Suddenly, she saw Strawgirl, frantically waving her straw arms. Maybe opened the window. 'Quick!' panted Strawgirl. 'Men here. Want cows.'

Maybe quickly pulled on her blue jeans and a black jumper. She pushed her feet into her trainers – no socks, no time for socks. 'Show me, Strawgirl,' she said. Her heart was in her mouth. If anything happened to her cows, she would kill for them. She would. She didn't care if she ended up in prison. She would kill anybody who hurt her cows.

'What about that one?' Jimmy suggested, pointing to Madame Bovary. Now he was in the strongest position, it was down to him to pull this whole thing off and scoop up the accolade. He pointed at the big cow to his right.

Jimmy used to work on a farm and he knew how

160

to handle cows. He had never told the twins this because he liked to keep things back so that he could surprise people. Jimmy talked softly to the animal and walked behind her. He stood, speaking quietly, not doing anything at all, quite some distance from Madame Bovary. The twins exchanged a look. Harold thought, Come on, man, we haven't got all night, but he said nothing. Arnold was delighted to get a bit of breathing space. In fact, Arnold wouldn't mind if Jimmy read the cow all of *War and Peace*.

Jimmy approached Madame Bovary slowly, still walking behind her. 'That's it. Don't be afraid,' he said. He got behind her and grabbed hold of her tail near the root, then he held it up vertically. 'Now, to get this beast to move, you just have to curl the tail like so.' He began to curl the tail carefully in a flat coil against her rump. The cow moved forward willingly. Jimmy whispered the whole time. 'That's it, you great big beast. Clever big coo. Come on. This way. Aye, aye. You're doing fine. Through here noo, broon coo. That's it. Through this gate here.'

Maybe and Strawgirl hid behind the trees, watching the three big men in long black coats. 'Same men,' Strawgirl whispered, pointing at the twins.

'What are we going to do?' Maybe said, clutching at Strawgirl. By the time they woke up Irene and she called the police, the men would be gone. There was nothing for Maybe and Strawgirl to do except follow them.

*

Harold and Arnold watched Jimmy get the cow through the gateway in total astonishment. It looked easy, the way he was doing it. He stood back from the gate so that he didn't put the cow off or get in the way. He made his arms big, extending them with branches. When Madame Bovary tried to turn back, he simply shook the branches.

'My God! The man's a genius!' Harold said admiringly.

Maybe exchanged a look with Strawgirl. 'That man knows how to handle cows,' she said. 'Who has he got, can you see?'

Strawgirl used her night vision to read the tag round the cow's neck. 'Madame Bovary,' she said.

'Oh, no, Madame Bovary!' Maybe gulped, though Strawgirl knew she would react like that with all of her cows.

So far, so good. Jimmy led the cow towards the trailer. 'Over to you, boys,' he said, knowing he was not going to be able to persuade the cow into the horsebox. The ramp was too high, and they hadn't covered it with sand to stop the cow slipping, or sprinkled it with straw to make her feel safe. Jimmy hadn't told the twins to do this because he felt torn about stealing the cows in the first place.

Harold and Arnold stared at each other, one face perfectly reflecting the alarm of the other. 'Oh, come on, Jimmy,' Arnold said. 'You've got the touch.'

'Naw. You two do this bit. You've got to earn your money too. I'm no' doing everything. I'm no' a mug.'

Harold got the rope out and tried to throw it round the cow's backside. He tried to heave her forward. Madame Bovary cried out in fright. She cut Jimmy a pleading look. Jimmy turned away and lit up an imaginary cigar. He puffed out into the night air. The smoke trailed its way up and up like strings from a kite.

Harold tried to put the rope round the cow's neck and pull it like a type of halter. This worked a little and the cow moved up the ramp. But the tinny din her hooves made on the steel alarmed her and she mooed again. 'Oh, God!' Jimmy got behind her and pushed and pushed. 'Don't let her get her head down for heaven's sake!' he shouted. 'Or she'll go down and refuse to budge.' Harold and Arnold went each side of the cow's head and pulled and pulled on the rope. Madame Bovary's legs scrambled and collapsed, banging on the ramp, but finally she managed it. She was trapped inside the trailer.

It had taken them one and a half hours; ninety minutes; five thousand and four hundred seconds. It had seemed a very long time.

Harold lifted up a loose fold of skin behind the cow's shoulder and slid the needle into the hollow he had created. The cow started. But he had managed to sedate her. She should sleep now till the morning when she would be more docile.

Jimmy spotted the nametag around her neck.

'Look at this,' he said. 'This cow is called Madame Bovary. What kind of name is that? Eh? It's no Daisy anyway, is it?'

'It's ridiculous to give the beasts names when they are going to get slaughtered,' Arnold said.

Harold was trying to remember who wrote *Madame Bovary*.

'Ah, but *they* weren't going to slaughter their beasts,' Jimmy said. 'It's *us* that are going to slaughter them.'

'Not us personally!' shrieked Arnold.

'Aye, us personally,' Jimmy said. 'In the sense that we are personally responsible for these here two coos' deaths. We will take them to the abattoir. We're no taking them to the beach for the day.'

'Yes, but we're not killing them with our own bare hands,' Arnold said, relieved. Jimmy was so dramatic.

'Perhaps we should,' Jimmy said. 'Then we'd know if we were up to it. You shouldn't be allowed to get other people to do your dirty work. We should do it ourselves.'

'Stop talking nonsense and focus on the task at hand!' Harold said, irritated.

'To think we've got to do that all over again,' Arnold said, close to tears.

'And again and again,' his twin said, 'if the Mac-Phersons don't see sense.'

'Right, boys, let's get going,' Jimmy said. 'We better capture another coo.'

'Let's take this one back to the castle first and come back,' Harold said.

Up on the roof of the trailer, lying flat facing the vast expanse of night sky, Maybe and Strawgirl held their breath, silent and scared. The sky was a dark blanket filled with jewels, glittering, sparkling and fizzing with light, chips of diamonds. Maybe looked up at the night sky amazed at its miraculous beauty. It was impossible to imagine that anything horrible could happen under such an astonishing display of stars.

28

Madame Bovary

Madame Bovary had never felt so heavy in her cow self all her cow life. Not even when she was carrying her calf, Barnes, who was sent away because he was a boy calf. At home, they were all females. The bulls-to-be had to go. Her legs ached and when she tried to stand, they shook – thin bones with an inch deep of skin. She was awake, but not awake. She was asleep, but not asleep. Her eyes were half-open, but everything that she could see was blurred. A thick mist covered everything: the stone cobbles, the stables, the house, the people.

Her sense of smell was still working properly, though. She could smell that something was wrong. She was far from home. There was no nice aroma of warm hay, no lovely green fresh grass, no pure scent of spring water. Here, the smells she breathed through her wide cow nostrils frightened her. The sour smell of strange men, the musty dank of the castle walls, the oil and diesel from the trailer. It was cold under her cow body. The old, cold cobbles in the stables dug into her skin.

Madame Bovary was dizzy and alone. She had never been on her own before without any of her herd. She sensed that there was nobody in the world that was known to her, not a single familiar smell or sound. Even the air here tasted different on her thick cow tongue.

There were no cows to give a back-rub to, back-to-back, or to help switch flies off her bottom, tail to tail. No cows to run with, to lie down with in the pasture, to graze and ruminate with in a glad group over life and its pleasures. No mutual grooming sessions, no mutual tail-switching. The whole point, the entire purpose of living, had been stripped from Madame Bovary's hide. For the first time in her life, she was utterly alone. It was terrifying. It felt so wrong, she thought she might die. She could feel her own death closing in on her, like the gates of a slaughterhouse.

Madame Bovary let out a sad, jerky breath from her pink mouth. She drifted off again, out into the bleak oblivion of drugged sleep. Way away in the distant background, she heard the noises of this new world. She tried to rouse herself, but couldn't. It wasn't even possible for her to take a drink of water. She had no strength. Now that she had no herd to live for, nobody to love, she had no willpower either. All of her sparkle, the bright light that shone in her eyes as she swung her wide hips from side to side and spun her tail around, was gone. Madame Bovary was all jittery now – nerves and hooves, flapping ears and switching tail.

29

Night Visit

Strawgirl and Maybe hid behind the wall of the stables at Cull Castle. They watched the trailer take off again for Wishing Well Farm. That gave them some time to snoop around and see what the men intended to do next. It was Maybe who spotted the unmarked animal transport vehicle. 'I follow same men,' Strawgirl said. 'Maybe wait. I follow.'

'I want to come too!' Maybe insisted.

'No. Not safe,' Strawgirl said. 'Don't see Strawgirl. See Maybe.'

'Why don't we set Madame Bovary free while they are away?' Maybe said, through tears.

'No, later.'

Maybe wondered if Strawgirl's confidence was justified. What if Madame Bovary were slaughtered? What if there were nothing at all that they could do to save her? What if Wishing Well Farm were destroyed? It seemed to Maybe that they would be defeated. For a moment, standing there against the castle wall, Maybe lost faith – faith in her ability to ever manage to keep her farm.

What could she do? This minute, she could go and talk to Madame Bovary. 'I'm going to see her,' Maybe said to Strawgirl. Maybe walked softly towards her cow. She was tethered to a post in the old stables.

Cows are not dogs, they will never wag their tails or jump on you to show how excited they are to see you, yet Maybe had never seen such a look of excitement and relief in Madame Bovary's eyes. She rubbed her face against her beautiful brown-and-white cow. She patted the sides of her body. 'I promise you, I'm going to save you,' she whispered. Madame Bovary seemed calmer now that she had seen Maybe. Maybe leaned against the cow's warm flank, suddenly overcome with exhaustion. She slumped to the floor and fell asleep.

Hardly any time had passed at all when Strawgirl shook Maybe awake. 'Hurry! Hide. I follow. Hurry!' Strawgirl took Maybe's hand and ran behind the stable wall. Maybe slipped and fell on the wet cobble-stones.

'What was that noise? the Glaswegian voice said.

'I didn't hear anything,' one of the twins said.

'Well, I did. Let me just look here.'

Maybe and Strawgirl crept along the end of the wall. 'Down,' Strawgirl whispered. She could always camouflage herself, but Maybe was at a distinct disadvantage.

They lay down, pressing themselves into the stone. A beam from a torch flashed near them, but not, thankfully, on them. Maybe felt as if she would explode from holding her breath in for so long. 'Please,' she begged silently. 'Please don't find us.' She closed her eyes tight. She crossed her fingers in the dark. She couldn't bear to look. If she looked and saw a man approaching, she would pass out.

The sound of men's boots came very close. 'What's that?' she heard one of them say. 'That bundle there.' She heard the boots moving towards her. Strawgirl squeezed her hand. The torch flashed on them. She could sense the light even with her eyes shut.

'It's nothing,' she heard the Glasgow voice say. 'Just a pile of straw.'

Relief made Maybe let out a long breath. Strawgirl pinched her. 'Sssssh.' They heard the footsteps walk off in the other direction.

Madame Bovary heard a sound that was known to her; one of the men coughed. Through the freakish early light a thing appeared – a big thing, swaying. She was being pulled along by the big men. The smell hit Madame Bovary's nostrils. It was another cow! Oh, rejoice and be thankful. Company. Another cow.

She looked up and tried to scramble to her feet. Her vision cleared a little and the cold air rushed to her head. She knew this cow. Out of the corner of her brown eye, Madame Bovary watched the poor beast being pulled and dragged, as she must have been pulled and dragged, to the stalls where horses had once been kept. She was not from Madame Bovary's inner circle, but she was from her big herd. For that Madame Bovary was grateful. She stared at the men. There were the two same tall men with the blond hair and the sharp noses. There was the smaller one with the brown hair. She watched them closely as they tied up her companion. Oh, she would remember them.

The men led Madame Bovary and Memphis Minnie into the unmarked vehicle. Memphis moaned a deep, long noise of protest, but they still managed to get both the cows into this new, strange darkness and bang the doors shut.

'I follow. You stay,' Strawgirl hissed urgently. She flew off. Maybe stood, trembling. She didn't want Strawgirl to leave her on her own. She wanted to be with Strawgirl the whole time. With Strawgirl, Maybe felt no harm would come to her. By herself, she feared for her own safety.

At least the sun was beginning to rise slowly in the east. A huge bright-red ball floated slowly up the sky as if the sky were a long river and the sun a red balloon. The sky was still dark apart from the flame-red sun. It was cold, freezing cold. Maybe rubbed her arms up and down to try and keep warm.

30

The Abattoir

Strawgirl streaked through the air, twirling and swirling though the morning mist and the clouds. She followed the trailer down the winding road. Sometimes, she had to hang about in the sky, waiting for the men down below to catch up. She floated then on the spot, like some clouds do for a long time, like a great heron in the sky, flying without seeming to move, flapping its large expanse of wing. Usually Strawgirl was happy when she flew, up, up, up in the wonderful white blossom of cloud. Free. But this morning, this early, she was more troubled than she had ever been.

Swirling above the men as they negotiated a tight hairpin bend with the trailer, she cut across the top of Ben Hope and over Loch na Seilg. She flew over the snow-capped top of Ben Loyal, south of Tongue. She soared above the Kinlock river, over the top of a waterfall where the water threw itself over the cliff, and rushed headlong down into an unfathomable, deep pool. Flying right above the trees, she could see some bald patches where there were no leaves. The heather had spread over the hills, purple and lush.

Strawgirl had grown so attached to Maybe she loved everything about her. The way her black curls framed her face, her deep, dark eyes like the brown pools at the bottom of the waterfall. The way her skin shone and shimmered. The way she spoke. Her silver rings, her long fingers. The fancy pins for her hair. Her clothes. Most of all, Strawgirl loved the way that Maybe was standing up for her farm. She had guts.

Suddenly, Strawgirl looked down and saw that the trailer had stopped. A sign read: *Private Land. Trespassers will be prosecuted.* Two massive, grey metal doors hung like iron curtains at the entrance to the abattoir. One of the men jumped out of the vehicle and pushed open the heavy doors. Quickly, Strawgirl climbed up a sycamore, the nearest tree to the abattoir's opening. Committing the place to memory, she took one more look around, trying to make everything special and unique. There was that particular bend, the way the hills dipped in the middle over there, the cluster of one, two, three, four, five sycamore trees, that huge oak behind them, the way the path into the abattoir was muddy and worn. Positive that she would remember this place, Strawgirl climbed on to a huge rock and flew off.

She had a terrible feeling that something bad had happened to Maybe, but perhaps that was because she loved her so much. When you love somebody, you worry – simple as that. As she flew back the way she had come, past the waterfall, the bend of the Kinlock, over the top of Ben Hope, she hoped against hope that her instinct was wrong, that it was only love making her fret.

Strawgirl arrived back at Cull Castle before the brothers and Jimmy. She found Maybe lying in the stables, asleep. Perhaps that was why Strawgirl had worried about her so much, it had seemed as if Maybe's light had gone out. While Maybe was asleep, Strawgirl hadn't been able to pick up her thoughts and feelings.

'Wake, Maybe,' she whispered urgently. 'We go.'

Maybe was startled. For a moment, she couldn't remember where she was. She looked around herself and groaned. The men had two of her cows already. They would take more. She would have to go home and convince her mother to phone the police. They would have to act quickly or the cows would be killed. She remembered what the note had said about 'slaughter days', the second Friday of the month. It was Sunday night tonight. Maybe had four days to rescue her cows.

It was daylight now. The red ball of the sun had turned to a pale-yellow one. There was a fresh, clean smell of autumn. The leaves were weeping from the trees, the birds twittering. Nature was still going on. Nothing had stopped. The sky was still the sky. The ground was still under her feet. It all seemed so bizarre to Maybe, as if she personally had been picked for this particular nightmare. Where or when was it all going to end? She tried to imagine that Sergeant Pawlinski believed her. How could she explain that she knew her cows were in an abattoir? Maybe shivered. It was frightening when adults didn't believe you. It made you feel helpless and hopeless. She doubted whether she and Strawgirl were going to be enough. She looked at Strawgirl's bright eyes. It seemed as if Strawgirl was reading her thoughts. 'Trust me,' she said.

Then they took off, the two of them – the girl made of straw and the girl made of flesh and blood – up, up, up into the sky, heading south-west for Wishing Well Farm, through the clouds. Maybe remembered learning at school that if clouds could be weighed, they would weigh hundreds of tonnes. You would never imagine, flying through clouds, that they were so heavy. They felt so light, so airy. It seemed to Maybe as if she were flying through her own dream.

Later, Maybe fell fast asleep in the comfort of her own single bed, next to the window. She had two hours before she would need to get up and milk her cows. In the morning, she would need to convince her mum to do something, to call the police.

31

Spider

'Molly?' Ms Rose said. 'Are you listening?'

'Yes, Ms Rose,' Molly said, shuffling in her seat.

But, of course, Maybe wasn't listening. She was frantically worrying about her cows. Her mother had made her go to school that morning, promising she'd count the cows and ring the police if there were any missing. But Maybe wasn't sure she would. Her mother often said she would do things and then she forgot, or lost interest. Her mother wasn't the reliable, dependable person she used to be. And there were only four days left! Four days to save Madame Bovary and Memphis Minnie.

'Go ahead then,' Ms Rose said. 'Continue reading where Troy left off.'

Troy sniggered because it was obvious that Molly hadn't taken anything in. Nothing was more delicious than watching your enemy get told off. It was so nice; you played it back to yourself in your mind – your own personal rewind.

'Molly MacPherson!' Ms Rose said. The anger was

rising step by step. 'I hope you've been paying attention.' It was some time now since Molly's dad had died. Ms Rose felt that Molly was playing on her sympathy, using his death as an excuse not to try her best at school.

Troy noticed Molly's index finger swivel round and round. Her finger dropped to the very spot in the book as if it had been led by somebody else. Troy couldn't believe it. 'Thomas . . .' continued Molly, starting to read at just the right place in *Thomas Kempe*.

'Och, rabies,' Troy said to himself. 'The nasty lassie's got away with it again.'

'Thank you, Molly,' Ms Rose said, gratefully. Her voice was warm, as if acknowledging that she had made a mistake. 'Your reading has improved. I'm awful pleased with you, so I am. And you put a nice bit of expression into your voice there.' Maybe's face shone like a gold star, the teacher's praise suffusing her skin till a warm glow glinted under the brown. She didn't need to turn around to know that Troy was looking at her. His eyes were boring two small smoky holes in her back.

Ever since the day they had to run away from Molly MacPherson's farm, Troy had been itching to get his revenge. It was a matter of a loss of face. You couldn't let a girl beat you, but worse still, you couldn't let a girl's geese beat you. The farm was not a good place to stage Round Two. Troy still had a horror of those geese that day, their terrible flapping wings, their alarming honking, their bright, greedy, beady eyes, and, most terrifying of all, their orange beaks, opening and closing around his frightened flesh.

It had to take place in the school really, in a part of the school where it would be easy to capture her – somewhere hardly anybody went to. How to lure her there though, that was the problem. 'We'll need to bribe somebody she trusts,' Troy told Moron during the morning break. 'That Lizzie. She'll do.'

'Aye. Right. No problem,' Moron said. 'What will I say?'

Spider said, 'Can we not leave her alone. Her dad died. I mean, her dad DIED.'

'So?' Troy said.

'Well, it's not nice is it – to have a dad die,' Spider said sulkily.

'How would you know?' Troy asked.

'Well, my dad's as good as dead. I mean, I never see him.'

'So? You've got a stepdad,' Troy said impatiently.

'He's horrible,' Spider said. Spider had never got on with his mum's new partner and blamed him for the fact that he never got to see his dad. He hated seeing the guy with his arm round his mum. It felt wrong. It should be his mum and dad together. Parents shouldn't break up once they've made you, Spider thought. It seemed to him that his mum wasn't interested in him any more. She only cared about his stepdad. At night, Spider dreamed of his dad – the times they used to fish together in the loch and catch perch or pike.

'Look, we better hurry up. The bell's gonna go,' Moron said. 'What's the plan, wee men?'

'Here's the plan,' Troy said as it flashed in front of his eyes, the most perfect, calculating manipulation he had created to date. 'I think I'm going to join the police force when I grow up,' he said. 'I think I'll be really talented at setting people up – you know, laying traps and that, planting evidence. Oh, that'd be a pure dead brilliant job, so it would.'

Moron's face lit up, sheer admiration switching on the bulb. 'Can I be your deputy?' he said as Spider shrugged his shoulders.

At lunchtime, a strange thing happened in the dinner hall. Spider jumped the queue and stood in front of Maybe. 'Nice one!' shouted Troy from the hotplates section.

'Life is too short,' Maybe said to herself. Life was too short to get stressed when somebody jumped the queue. What was the point? You only made yourself agitated and angry and they never went to the back of the queue, anyway. So Maybe ignored Spider. Perhaps that was why she was all the more surprised to find him turning and whispering urgently to her, 'Watch your back tonight! Don't trust Lizzie.' Maybe frowned. Then he said, in a loud voice, 'What are you staring at? Want a photo?' Moron and Troy snorted with laughter and pushed in to join him, their plates full of chips, beans and sausages. Maybe had a cheese salad, a black cherry yogurt and a glass of water.

'Look at the state of that plate,' Moron said. The idea of not having chips was painful.

'People who actually choose salad need their heads looking at,' Moron said, staring at Maybe's head. The Tongs went and sat down at a table. As she passed them, Maybe saw Spider smile at her. 'It gets increasingly difficult these days to work out what is going on,' Maybe thought to herself. So it was, too.

Past experience had taught Maybe when the Tongs were up to something. It was to do with the look on their faces, the way they tried to act casual and conceal their excitement, the way they looked at her quickly and, when she looked back, looked away. She knew, she knew, she knew. If only Strawgirl could come to school with her, then she would be protected. She could fly. She could walk through the walls: from her classroom to the corridor, through the school hall, through that wall, and out into the playground. It might have been possible then to stand on top of the bicycle-shed roof and take off, though she wouldn't actually have liked her enemies or even her friends to see her fly. Odd though it was, she would have felt a bit shy, flying through the sky with them dumbfounded in the playground, grounded, looking up at her – gormless, gobsmacked, green with envy.

Maybe was one of those people who like to keep their talents hidden; if she was good at something, she would rarely boast. She had a beautiful singing voice, but she wouldn't join the choir. She would never sing when her mum and dad had parties, so nobody knew what a lovely voice she had except her parents. A little modest smile, a shy fluttering of the eyelashes, a spring in her step, might give her away, but only to those who knew her well. Yes, flying felt private.

It was all fantasy anyway, because Strawgirl was not here. Try as she might to concentrate on the geography lesson – Ms Rose was talking to them about coal mines, about the layers and levels that are down a pit before you get to the shining black coalface – Maybe's mind wandered. All she could think about was her cows trapped at the abattoir and how she must rescue them. Ms Rose was telling them how difficult it was for children in the past who had to work for a living, and how very small children were sent down the mine because they could crawl along the coalface quite easily. Maybe listened for a moment, fascinated by the children of history. Ms Rose talked of their lungs filling with coal dust and how the mine owners took enormous risks with the children's lives just to make money.

She thought of her cows. How unscrupulous farmers made huge profits from cows, from keeping them in overcrowded barns, from transporting them in overcrowded vehicles. She thought how proud her father had been of Wishing Well, how he treated his cows to a decent life, good food and kindness. Right now, at this moment, Memphis and Madame Bovary were at the abattoir. Maybe thought of her mother's blank expression, and her confidence in her faltered. It was as if Irene had wandered quietly back into the strange, thick depression. As if she had just walked off into a wardrobe dense with clothes and Maybe couldn't reach her. She couldn't pull her out. She couldn't make her real.

Later that morning, Maybe had told Annie and Fred about the brothers' scheme. They were dubious too, but said they would count the cows and check if there were any missing and, if there were, would get her mum to phone the police. That was how things had been left. Maybe hoped she would go home to find that the police had recaptured their cows and brought them back to the farm.

The minutes ticked by, fast as a teacher's swift red ticks, because the story of the children of the mines was riveting. Time rushed past and the school day was suddenly, surprisingly, over. It was time to pack the bag, put the blazer on and wait for the school bus, all over again. Hard to believe, the way the day slid down a shaft sometimes, from morning light at the top, to dark night at the bottom.

Lizzie Gordon, a plump girl, small in height for her age, with light-brown hair, brown eyes and freckles, appeared at Maybe's side. 'Is it your birthday, Molly?' she asked.

'No,' Maybe said, guardedly. 'Why?'

'Oh, because there's a surprise for you in the cloakroom.'

'For me?'

'Yep.'

'Who says?'

'Angie told me.'

'Who told Angie?'

'I don't know, Molly. What's wrong? I'd be chuffed if somebody told me I had a surprise.'

'There can be nice surprises and nasty ones,' Maybe said.

'Yes, but this is a birthday surprise,' Lizzie said, perplexed. Maybe was so strange.

'Yeah, well how come it's not my birthday?'

'Well, they've maybe got the date wrong, but you could still accept the prezzie.'

Maybe looked up to see Moron walking towards her. 'We've decided to make friends with you,' Moron said. 'We've got you a present to say we're sorry.'

'I thought it was a birthday present,' Lizzie said, confused.

'Well, it's not,' Moron said, quite viciously.

The way he snapped at Lizzie was the proof Maybe needed. Of course they didn't want to make friends; they wanted to get even. How brainless of her to believe them, even for a split second! Spider had warned her about Lizzie. Now why had Spider done that? 'Oh! I've forgotten my homework,' Maybe said, running back towards her classroom. She raced up the two flights of wide stairs to her classroom, room eleven. She banged open the door and rushed to her desk, pretending to sift through the mess until she heard footsteps on the stairs.

She came out of the classroom a second later and looked left, then right. At the top of the stairs she tried to look right down to see if anybody was waiting below. She spotted Troy's black shoe with the steel toecap on the bend of the stairs. She rushed back to her classroom and opened the window. It was a long way down, right enough, but there was no choice. She climbed out of the window, shimmied up the drainpipe on to the roof and crawled along the slates. There was no way she was letting those boys beat her up; she needed all her strength to rescue her cows.

In the distance she could hear Troy shout, 'The window's open. She must be on the ROOF!' She steadied herself, standing up. Heights didn't frighten her any more. Which one of them would have the bottle to follow her up on to the roof? She turned around. On the other side of the roof, Troy was running towards her followed by Moron, followed by Spider.

Panic hit her like a heavy slap of wind. It hadn't even occurred to her how to get down. She ran right to the edge and looked over. It was much too high to jump. She ran further on and jumped down one floor until she was on the roof of the school hall. It was still too high to jump all the way to the ground.

A whole group of children had gathered below and were standing looking up. Two teachers were there now too. One of them shouted, 'You must stay where you are. It is dangerous. We'll call the fire brigade.' At one point in her life it would have been thrilling to think of being rescued from a roof by firemen, but she was past that stage now. It would be too late by the time they arrived.

Maybe ran along the grey roof. Her feet hit a couple of loose slates and they slid down, shattering on the playground. A girl below just managed to dodge a falling slate. 'That could have cracked my skull!' Rhona shouted, her voice full of indignation and wonder. Maybe slipped and slid down the roof, nearly falling right off it. She managed to grab on to the edge by her nails. She clung on for dear life, her body swinging from side to side. The people down below let out a collective gasp. Troy was not far behind Maybe. Neither was Spider, but Moron was way behind, out of breath.

Maybe gripped the edge of the roof, her fingers aching. Any minute now she would have to let go. She would probably break a leg. She might even break her neck. She might die. Spider was above her. 'Give me your hand!' he shouted. 'It's your only hope.' Maybe didn't trust him. The choice was between the devil and the deep blue sea. Maybe stretched a hand out towards Spider and he pulled her. He couldn't manage – she was too heavy. 'Give me a hand here,' he ordered Troy. And Troy did; he actually helped. Perhaps he helped because there was a big audience down below and he didn't want anybody to see him hurt Maybe. Bullies never like to be watched. Spider took one hand and Troy took the other and they both pulled and dragged and heaved Maybe back on to the roof.

Next thing: the headmistress's office. Moron, Spider, Troy and Maybe were trying to explain their animosity, their rivalry, their antagonism for one another. The headmistress was allowing each to have their say about the day's outlandish events. When she went to reprimand Maybe for leading them all up on the roof in the first place, it was Spider who intervened. 'It was my fault, Miss Monument,' he admitted. Troy glared at him, and Moron's jaw dropped open. Spider wasn't exactly betraying Troy, yet Troy was still evidently furious. Maybe felt even more worried. Without meaning to, Spider had given Troy another reason to loathe Maybe. Troy stared at her, his face stony with silence. Maybe looked away. That look, filled as it was with spite and hatred, horrified her, even in the sanctuary of the headmistress's study.

Maybe glanced at Spider. He looked back. He didn't smile but nor did he look as if he hated her. In fact, Spider looked as if he might feel sorry for her. His face was red from all the effort on the roof and his eyes were watery. Maybe couldn't understand him. One minute he was chasing her; the next he was standing up for her. Put it this way: some things are just plain weird, Maybe thought. She noticed that

Spider's ears were red. She looked down at her shoes. They were all scuffed from the roof-chase.

'I'm not convinced it was your fault, Steven,' Miss Monument said. 'It is obviously against the school rules for anybody to be up on the roof, so all of you will be punished. If I have any more trouble I will be calling in your mothers and fathers.' She looked at Maybe and remembered that her father had died, and felt a moment's awkwardness. 'I will speak to a parent,' she said, a little flustered.

'We will not tolerate any kind of intimidation at this school, nor will we tolerate those who think they can just run up on the roof to escape things, rather than come and discuss them. If you have any problems in the future, Molly MacPherson, you see me!' she said. She sounded angry with Maybe, as if she had brought the bullying on herself. Why didn't adults understand that telling on bullies only made matters worse?

Miss Monument excused them from her study, giving them all an essay to write on the importance of school rules.

Maybe left her office and rushed for the bus stop. On the way, she glanced back at the school roof. A line of grey wood pigeons sat there now. They seemed to be telling each other the news.

32

Way to Go

Since Jamie died, Irene MacPherson had found it difficult to motivate herself. Nothing seemed to matter any more. She was later than usual getting up, and later still going to bed. Her sleep was disturbed by nightmares. Sometimes she didn't get herself dressed until just before Maybe came home from school. Her hair wasn't washed with anything like her usual regularity. Nor did she bother about what she wore; she pulled on what was nearest and what was most comfortable. It was a long time since Irene MacPherson had worn earrings or a bangle or a pin for her hair or high heels or make-up or a silk scarf. Or anything with any colour at all. She dressed in blacks and charcoal greys and dark browns and navy blues.

The same went for cooking. She just couldn't be bothered. Maybe did most of it now, and it was all Irene could do to muster the strength to eat. The old Irene would have been shocked and surprised at this new Irene – this dull, sad, languid, pale woman with no get-up-and-go, no spark, no ideas. This new

Irene didn't even stop to ask herself what had happened to the old one. A light inside had gone out, and she was just going through the motions. Living. Sleeping. Eating. If it wasn't for Maybe, she could not say what she might have done to herself. But Maybe at least kept the clock ticking, the heart beating, the blood circulating round the body and the body moving from living room to bathroom to bedroom, day in, day out.

This particular day Irene went downstairs at noon. It was heavy and gloomy outside, still quite dark. The day was as bleak as Irene's thoughts. She sighed to herself. Her sighs were the only noise in the house. She made herself a cup of tea. Maybe had brought her one that morning which was sitting, untouched and cold, upstairs by her bed, a skin like a mask formed on top, waiting for Maybe to come home. Maybe had been all agitated that morning about the cows. Irene thought her daughter was losing her balance. She felt guilty that she had been neglecting her. Last night had given her the shock of her life: to go into Maybe's bedroom and find her gone. Irene blamed herself for not being a good mum. She would need to put Maybe first. She'd need to try and put Jamie behind her.

The post was sitting on the table alongside Saturday's post and the post of the days before that. Irene's eyes glanced over it in a desultory fashion. She was about to put it all on the mantelpiece for later when her eyes fell on a photograph of Jamie, Maybe and herself when Maybe was three years old. The photograph had been taken on a family holiday to the Isle of Mull, near Calgary Bay. Irene smiled for a moment to herself. Jamie's eyes in the photograph had the same intensity as his living eyes, and for a moment Irene was shocked by how real Jamie looked. It was an odd thing when somebody died to have them real like this before you, holding a bucket and a spade, wearing green swimming trunks, smiling and with bare feet, almost as if time had heard nothing about the death.

Irene picked up the photograph, letting the letters fall at her feet. She stared at Jamie for the longest time. 'You are dead now,' she told the photograph. 'You really are, aren't you? You are dead.' She started to cry properly for the first time since Jamie's death. It was as if she had kept her tears inside her for months. When they came out, they splashed down her face, salty and copious – weeks and weeks of tears. Her cries became louder and louder. 'You are dead. You are dead! *Dead, dead, dead.*' She wanted to rip the photograph up because it was telling a lie – it was pretending that Jamie was alive when he wasn't. But the photograph knew nothing of the future. It was a moment, a single lovely moment, in that wonderful holiday they had all had together.

Suddenly galvanized into action, Irene rushed around the house, collecting all the photographs where Jamie appeared, collecting his football medals and his certificates. She packed them up in an old suitcase. First she lined the case with a soft flannel sheet, and then she put all the paraphernalia inside. Then she pulled all of Jamie's clothes out of their wardrobe: his shirts, his ties, his trousers, his jumpers. She put them in big black bin bags. Then she threw out his shoes, his brown leather ones, his black ones, his trainers. When she was finished, her eyelids were swollen and puffy as slugs; her face was washed out and her eyes were still glistening with tears like pools enlivened by the rain. But something in her had lifted. Something felt better. For the first time since Jamie had died, Irene brushed her hair and washed her face, putting some cream on her cheeks. It was a start.

When Maybe returned from school she would be delighted to find her mother washed, presentable and fresh looking, as if she had just walked through a tunnel and out, out, into the pale afternoon light.

But the minute Irene MacPherson looked at the post, her face changed. An eviction notice. Another eviction letter. She rifled through the entire pile as if she had never seen a letter like that before. Her face clouded over. A memory came back to her of the letter that had come the day before Jamie's death. A fresh anger glowed now on her cheeks, fiery and indignant. She must enlist the help of the villagers. The local Spar shop wouldn't be pleased to hear about Domino Supermarkets, nor would the greengrocer's or the butcher's. She must start to do something. She must count her cows. Perhaps her daughter was right after all.

Irene felt shocked at her own indifference. It was as if she had suddenly woken up from a very long dream, like somebody in a fairy tale, except that Irene felt that she had woken up into a nightmare. Now Irene understood Maybe's desperation – the desperation that she had simply watched like a person watches a movie, passively. Now Irene shared Maybe's concern and walked straight out to the field to count her cows.

In the field, in the cold autumn day, the cows lay down on the ground. Evidently it was going to rain. Irene looked up at the sky. It was filled with dark-grey clouds that loomed like poisonous vapours over her head. They were filled with heavy rain; it was bunched up in those dark holes waiting for a chance to speak. For weeks after Jamie's death, Irene had kept in all of her tears. The rain clouds were the sky's tears. Soon they would fall. Soon they would soak everything. Irene went back inside the house and got out her black address book. She had a long afternoon's phoning ahead of her.

33

Jimmy Thinks Again

A day later, Harold checked his post and listened to his answering machine. There was no message from the MacPhersons.

'That's it!' said Harold. 'They haven't budged an inch. We still haven't received any information about their plans to shift their butts – not one iota.'

'Give them a bit more time,' Jimmy said. 'You've got to understand, this is people's livelihoods. This is their home. Wait another week.'

Harold shot Jimmy a look of total and utter disbelief.

'What's the look for?' Jimmy asked defensively.

'I'm looking like that,' said Harold icily, 'because you don't seem to get it.'

'Get what?' said Jimmy, his hackles rising. He was not going to stand around this couple of twerp twins and be accused of being stupid, of not being the full shilling. Jimmy was the full shilling all right.

'We need them to move now or the deal will collapse. No land. No development. We will have to steal four more cows tonight, and if that doesn't do it we'll take more. We might get them legally evicted. But that takes time. Going through the stupid courts takes ages. We need them to move *now*. Let's take four more of their cows tonight and get them to the abattoir. We need to terrorize them.'

'Wait till tomorrow night then, give them one more day,' Jimmy said.

'I mean, what do we need to *do* with these people?' Harold continued, outraged. 'Have a cow's head cut off and send it to them on a platter?'

It was Jimmy's turn to look at Harold. He was shocked.

'I dinny like the way you are talking,' Jimmy said, his voice rising with rage.

'Well, get the hell out then, you hypocrite,' Harold said.

Arnold intervened. 'Steady on, bro'. This man here was very good with the cows as I remember. We're not, are we? We're not good with cows.'

Jimmy was incensed at being called a hypocrite – furious because it contained the terrible truth. How could he involve himself in something like this just because he needed the money? Yes, he was angry with Harold, with Arnold, with his life so far for not being easy or lucky. But the person Jimmy was angry at most of all was himself.

He looked at Arnold, who was just standing there like an idiot ready to follow his twin brother's instructions. Arnold, who cared more about what Harold thought of him than he cared about what was right or wrong. Arnold, who was doing now what he had done all his life – copying his brother. As small boys, Jimmy imagined, the dynamic between these brothers would have been exactly the same: Harold kicked a ball, Arnold kicked a ball; Harold punched somebody, Arnold punched somebody. And here was Jimmy joining in. For what? For money. And what was Harold doing it for? Money. What else? Power. The thing that Harold enjoyed most about owning land was moving people off it. He wasn't the least bit unhappy about having to have the cows slaughtered. If anything, he was relishing the whole thing as if it was all a game, as if he had never managed to grow up.

Jimmy looked at the twins and felt distanced from them. They were still boys – boys who had grown up into men without empathy or conscience. But Jimmy did have a conscience. He did have a dim sense of what was right and what was not right, and this to him felt not right. No matter how many times Harold justified it by saying it was his land anyway, it still felt wrong to Jimmy. What do you do when you feel something is wrong? Do you keep on doing what you were going to do anyway? Or do you stop? Jimmy decided to stop. The game was up for him, money or no money. There had to be more to life than that. It occurred to him that, rather than just upping and leaving, he would be more effective if he continued to play along. Then he might stand some chance of helping the girl and her family before it was too late.

'Right then. Are you in?' Harold asked, challenging him. 'Then we'll agree on tomorrow night. Tomorrow night to steal four cows. We'll take it from there.'

There was something about Harold; people just said 'Yes' to him. Nobody dared to say 'No'. They just did what he wanted. There was never any discussion, really. It was the same about the smallest of things – what to have for breakfast or dinner, which pub to go to for a drink, what car to buy. Harold decided and everyone else agreed.

The world breaks down into types, Jimmy thought to himself. The decisive and the indecisive. The yes people and the no people. The window people and the aisle people. The poor people and the rich people. The leaders and the followers. 'Which am I?' Jimmy wondered. 'Am I a yes man or a no man?' He decided he would give Harold the shock of his life and become a no man. He would not do what Harold wanted. He would take off in the middle of the night and leave the MacPhersons a note, to warn them. Jimmy thought of his mother in her small council house in Glasgow. She wouldn't want a new wheelchair if she knew how he'd got it. But she would be proud of him now. Jimmy decided that tonight was the night he would not let money get the better of him. Tonight was the night that Jimmy Snell was going to join the human race.

There really wasn't much time to lose. Tomorrow

night they would be removing four more cows. The next night, eight more. The date set for the death of the cows at the abattoir was Friday. Soon that cow named Madame Bovary and the one called Memphis Minnie would die. Soon after, the rest of the herd would follow. The past couple of nights, Jimmy had found himself dreaming about Madame Bovary, her hooves slipping and sliding on the ramp of the trailer, her long moans into the night, her big cow eyes rolling about in her head, her anxious tail switching from side to side. In his dream, her fat cow tongue hung out of her mouth and frothy saliva dripped down her jaw. Then she collapsed and laid her wide, flat cow head next to his on the pillow. Jimmy would have liked to visit the cows, to talk softly to them and reassure them, to bring them some tasty cattle cake and tell them they were going to be saved. Somehow their big brown eyes had got to him. He could see them last thing before he fell asleep. They seemed to be imploring him, begging him not to do this.

And now here was Jimmy about to go back to Wishing Well that night, to look at the innocent cows standing there in the dark. Cows knew all about sadness, Jimmy thought. They could feel it like they could feel rain on their skin, like they could feel the grass under their hooves, the wind against their tails. Cows could sense sadness coming over the hills.

The moon was high up in the sky the night that Jimmy left Cull Castle and went to Wishing Well

Farm. He looked in at the sleeping twins, snoring in their bunk beds – could you believe it, grown men who still liked bunk beds – and was struck again by how similar they looked. It was two a.m. A clear night. The moon was patterned with wavy marble lines. A dark-blue circle of light surrounded it like an aura, like the moon's halo.

Jimmy tiptoed around the castle so as not to wake the twins. He pulled his clothes on and quietly walked down the stairs. He opened the door, which creaked a bit and made him hold his breath, then closed it. Once outside, Jimmy got on his motorbike and free-wheeled it down the hill so that it wouldn't wake them. A safe distance from the castle, he switched the engine on and roared off into the dark. It was the first time he had ridden his Kawasaki 750 for some time. In the pitch-blackness, with the one bright eye of his motorbike headlight lighting his path, the stars shining out their names, and the fresh night air rushing through his hair, Jimmy felt free for the first time in ages. He remembered exactly where to go. He knew the way even in the deep-purple darkness of the night. He hoped against hope that the brothers would not wake and find him gone.

Twenty minutes later, Jimmy's Kawasaki 750 was negotiating the bumpy farm road down to Wishing Well. It was the middle of the night, not a good time to leave a note, and how were they going to trust him now anyway? Perhaps he should try and wake the girl up, talk to her. His resolve started to weaken. Suddenly, he wasn't sure that this was a good idea at all. He could see the dark shape of the cows in the fields. He could sense them watching him, staring, just staring, the way cows do.

34

Moon

A full moon's face gaped in at Maybe's window. When she looked out she saw Strawgirl lying in the field, a heap of gold under the silver light. Maybe felt suddenly sad. Strawgirl was always looking up at the moon, pointing at it if it appeared in the sky before it was dark. Once Strawgirl had been beside herself with excitement when the sun and the moon had shared the same sky. 'Moon!' she'd shouted, and Maybe had had to squint up into the blue until her eyes found Strawgirl's thin fingernail of moon.

Since Strawgirl's arrival, Maybe started to notice the moon more. She found herself constantly looking up at it too, trying to think what else the moon looked like: a short straw, a hairclip, a clove of garlic, a wedge of lemon, the edge of a spider's web, a coin, a medal, an owl's eye.

After two full moons, it became clear to Maybe that Strawgirl was affected by the moon's tides. She was nervous or melancholy when it was full. When the moon was split in half, so cleanly it could have been cut by a knife, Strawgirl was wild, laughing, hysterical. When the moon bobbed behind the foaming clouds and raced the stars to the edge of the horizon, Strawgirl flew alongside it. 'Look!' she'd scream at Maybe when the moon made an appearance after hiding for ages behind clouds. 'It back!'

One night when the moon had been only a small half-smile in the darkening sky, Maybe had noticed that Strawgirl slept in exactly the same shape as the moon, her straw body curled into a comma. Another night when the moon had been sharp and curved like the blade of an ancient sword, a scimitar, Maybe had looked out of her window to see Strawgirl dancing in the fields, wild and violent. 'Moon!' she had shrieked, pointing up. And then it had looked like the yellow fang of a fox, a piece of apple, an orange, a salmon's back, an arched eyebrow.

Maybe would look at the moon as it pulled the oceans and seas over the surface of the land, dragging them behind it, far out in space, like a farmer in a distant field pulling his plough.

35

The Prisoner

Jimmy changed down gears as he approached the stables. His engine was a low groan, not a screaming roar. He sniffed the night air. He could smell the farm. It was such a clear night he could almost smell the stars. It was beautiful here in the dark, the low farm buildings blending with the land. The big moon like a face, watching. Jimmy looked up into the huge night sky. He took an imaginary cigar from his jacket and puffed imaginary smoke up into the galaxy. It was time for him to approach the house.

Just then, Jimmy got the shock of his life. Suddenly a long rope was being whipped around him at the speed of light. Under the bright moonlight, Jimmy felt as if he was caught up in a ferocious whirlwind. The whirl and the swirl and the twirl, the whip and the whisk and the waltz of the winding rope, left welts on his skin. He could feel it sting. It was so painful that Jimmy let out a cry. He couldn't stop himself. He felt himself being rolled up, furled, curled up. He was spinning round and round like a propeller.

Faster and faster, wrapping him and wrapping him, until Jimmy couldn't move his arms or his legs.

Even through his clothes the rope hurt, twisted around him so tightly he looked like a tornado. He was completely tied up, the rope tight as bandages round and round his body, from the top to the bottom, until he looked not unlike a mummy from Ancient Egypt.

He couldn't see anybody in the dark. There didn't appear to be anybody there. He couldn't even feel anyone's hand. All Jimmy could feel was the rip of rope. He was in agony. The rope had given him a good whipping. He was sure there would be rips, tears and welts all over his body tomorrow, if he ever got to see tomorrow. He had no idea what had happened to him.

Next thing, Jimmy found himself being dragged into the barn by an invisible force. Before he had a chance to examine himself in the dim light, he felt something brush across his cheek. Jimmy was terrified. Perhaps the place was haunted. Perhaps some ancient farm ghost had decided to exact its revenge. In two split seconds, something was pulled over Jimmy's head so that he could see nothing. He could still hear though. He could hear the gusty wind wheezing through the trees. He could hear bats flapping their wings. He could hear the woody flute of the barn owl and all kinds of scuttling and scraping noises. He could smell damp hay, cow dung and manure so strongly that he could taste the farm in his mouth.

His hands were tied tightly behind him and he could feel the sharpness of the rope cutting into him.

'What do you want, whoever you are?' Jimmy shouted. 'Tell me what you want, for God's sake.' Suddenly, he had a sensation of being left – of the thing or the spirit just leaving him, blindfolded and tied up as he was. 'You dinny understand. I'm here to help,' he mumbled.

He was lying curled up on a bale of hay. His feet were tied together, as were his legs and his arms. Jimmy was even more desperate to carry out his mission now that he was being thwarted. It had all crystallized for him. The right thing to do was warn these people about the destruction of the cows.

Jimmy worked on the blindfold first and managed to get it off by biting and pulling at it. I have lost my grip, he thought to himself, full of self-pity. Just when he was trying to be good, some strange force had to tie him up in a bloody barn. It was unreal, his life. He had been jinxed from the minute he came out of his mother's womb.

Once again, Maybe woke to the sensation of being shaken by Strawgirl.

'Prisoner!' Strawgirl said. Her voice sounded proud, proud as a cat that brings a dead dormouse to its dull owner.

Maybe woke up with a start. 'Who? Where? When? How?' These were the essential questions.

'Come,' Strawgirl said, holding out her straw hand. 'Barn.'

Maybe rushed her jeans on over her pyjamas in the dead of night. Oh, for a normal life. Oh, for an ordinary night's sleep, uninterrupted. When, oh when, would her life ever return to normal? She knew the answer to that question. It was 'Never.' Never, because her father was dead.

There in the barn was the 'prisoner' as Strawgirl had said. Maybe was impressed when she saw how tightly Strawgirl had tied him up, but she noticed that he'd managed to rip off his blindfold. But then it didn't matter if he saw them or not. There was nothing he could do. 'You'll cut off his circulation,' Maybe said. 'Let's loosen him a little.'

Jimmy stared at the dark girl. It was clear she was talking to somebody or something, but Jimmy couldn't see anything. She must be talking to the force that had tied him up. He should have known there was something strange about the girl from the time that she escaped from Cull's dungeon. Jimmy wished he could see an adult. He'd feel safer with an adult than with this freaky kid. 'Who are you talking to?' he asked.

'Strawgirl,' Maybe replied, pointing at her friend. Jimmy looked blank.

'Don't be silly. Look!' Maybe said, annoyed.

Jimmy said, 'I canny see anything but you and me in here.'

Maybe looked at Strawgirl. She was definitely there. She was real.

'Only you,' Strawgirl said.

'Only me?' Maybe said.

'Who are you talking to?' Jimmy asked. He could only hear Maybe's voice.

'Listen!' Maybe said, beside herself now. 'Strawgirl, say something!'

'Only you,' Strawgirl said again, a little sadly.

It was then that everything fell into place for Maybe. Not only could nobody else see Strawgirl, but also nobody else could hear her. She was invisible. She had no sound. Maybe grabbed Strawgirl's hand and made her take Jimmy's hand. 'I canny feel anything, except this blinking rope. Get if off me!' Jimmy said.

It explained a lot. It made Maybe think back. It was the reason that her mum had never seen Strawgirl in the house; the reason that Annie and Fred had never seen her in the field. It explained why the Tongs never commented on her the day they tried to set fire to the barn. Oddly, perhaps, Maybe felt upset that nobody else could see her Strawgirl. It made her wonder if Strawgirl was real or a figment of her imagination. She wanted everybody to be able to see her so that she could know for sure. 'No, of course you are real!' Maybe said to Strawgirl, working things out aloud.

'Only you,' Strawgirl repeated, lost for words. She was trying to tell Maybe something, but Maybe couldn't work out what it was. The wind whistled a high note. A bird fluttered to the top of the barn. A full moon waited outside the barn, way up in the sky, serene. It was a silent witness. Maybe looked out into the unreadable dark. She didn't know what to think any more. For a moment, it felt as if her whole world was falling apart. Everything that she had believed to be true was crumbling down. Nothing was real. Her dad had been alive and now he was dead. Strawgirl was visible to her and invisible to everybody else. But Jimmy sat here, tied up. That was real.

'Something tied me up!' Jimmy said. 'But I couldn't see anything. It was terrifying. And I came to help as well, so I did. I dinny come to steal any more coos.'

Maybe snapped out of her reverie and turned her attention to Jimmy. She felt the residual fury reinvent itself. How dare he steal her cows! At least he admitted it! Nobody else would believe her except her mother. Irene had contacted the police, but they seemed unconvinced. 'Nobody just steals two cows,' Sergeant Pawlinski had said. 'There must be some other explanation. They probably wandered off, or maybe you got the numbers wrong to begin with.' If she were anything like the bullies at her school, Maybe would punish Jimmy now and get pleasure from it.

'Look, wee girl,' Jimmy said, pleading. 'I've gone out of my way to come here.' (Maybe was furious at being called 'wee girl'.) 'This is for real. Those men I work with are coming tomorrow night to steal four more coos. They'll be here at midnight. I will be coming with them, but I won't be on their side. If you would just give me a chance to redeem myself here, I have an idea. I could help you. I haven't taken this decision lightly. I'm being totally honest here.' Jimmy resisted the impulse to swear in between 'totally' and 'honest'; he was talking to a young girl, after all. He had to mind his tongue.

Maybe considered what he was saying. Why would he say this if it weren't the truth? Or was this just an elaborate plan, a spectacular hoax? Perhaps he had been sent by the twins to pull just this kind of stunt. Maybe was not sure whether to trust the man Jimmy or not. She stared at his face. His deep, sunken eyes shone with the truth. She cut him free.

36

The Forest

Maybe climbed into her dirty green Land Rover and drove Strawgirl through her forest. Jimmy had told her they would be coming the back way into Wishing Well Farm tonight at midnight, along the forest road, in order to make sure nobody saw them. Maybe was driving through the forest at four o'clock in the afternoon so that she could plan her counter-attack. It came down to this: if you want something in life, you fight for it. You don't let it slide away from you. You don't say, 'There's nothing I can do about it,' and let the worst happen. There was plenty that Maybe could still do and she intended to do it. Since her dad died, it was down to her to look after the cows and the land. Maybe remembered her father as she looked after the land; she was tending to his spirit. She could find it everywhere: in a ploughed field, in the hay stacked neatly in the barn, in a field of oats, in a field of barley. Her father's working hands were all over the land, and the land now belonged to Maybe. It was up to her to save her farm in the name of her father.

The wheels of the Land Rover were caked with mud. Maybe had been driving for ages – now she was an expert. When her dad was alive, she was only allowed to drive the car on the farm road occasionally, but he'd always told her she had the knack. She was confident she could drive again. She moved the seat further forward than her dad did, but it was not too difficult to reach the pedals. Everyone said she had long legs for an eleven-year-old, and it wouldn't be long before she was as tall as her mum.

Wishing Well Farm covered 400 acres of land, 150 acres of which was forest – a Scots-pine forest, dense, loyal and secretive. The light was different here; the sunlight came through the trees, dappled and mysterious. On the forest floor lay millions of pine needles, like small tears the trees had shed in the night. There were few places on Wishing Well Farm that Maybe loved more than her forest. Here, in the dark heart of the farm, she felt special. It seemed as if the tall trees remembered her, had grown up with her. As a small child she called it her jungle. She could still see how it seemed to her then, huge and wild and thick and dark and never ending, like a fairy tale come to life. And she was the fairy tale's daughter. It smelled different in the forest too – fresh, mountain green, as if the trees had their very own perfume. The tall trees were good listeners; they had been on this farm for years, they belonged here where their roots lay tangled under the forest floor. They stood proud, seemingly invincible, in clusters, like dignified people attending a ceremony. When the wind came, they swayed together like dancers.

They had never seemed like just trees to Maybe, more like people. They had energy, they could love. Of course, her class would have collapsed in giggles if they saw her hug a tree, but on many a sad day Maybe had escaped into her forest and thrown her arms around one of her pines. She was convinced that hugging trees was good for you. And the tree had seemed to her to stand solid and comforting, whispering odd soothing sounds through its branches. So there was nothing worse for Maybe than to think of leaving her forest to live in a house in the nearest town. The idea of chopping all of her trees down to build a silly supermarket was sick and depraved – two of Maybe's favourite words.

Jimmy had told Maybe that the brothers planned to steal four cows, then eight, and then the whole lot. They were banking on the police's indifference and on the fact that the police respected their family name. People knew of old Mr Barnes-Gutteridge in Grumbeg. Jimmy told them that the brothers were corrupt and were operating many scams simultaneously. He said he wanted nothing to do with them any more. Jimmy had offered himself as a farmhand if the McPhersons kept the farm, if they managed to expose the brothers. He had helped them plan the counter-offensive.

Maybe hoped that she had made the right decision, trusting Jimmy. All decisions were painful, especially to Maybe, she who used to be so indecisive. There was always the possibility that the other option was the correct choice. There was always the little nagging voice – why didn't you go that way, not this? It was fork-in-the-road time and Maybe had chosen her path, rightly or wrongly; the choice was made now, it could not be undone. How different life would be, Maybe thought, if you could go around undoing the things you had just done; if you could take the path to your left instead of your right, after all.

Jimmy's eyes were honest eyes. They had stared straight back into Maybe's face. They were bright, alert. They did not look like the shifty eyes of a traitor – the stony, cold, dispassionate eyes of the deceiver. They looked like truthful eyes. Well, she hoped so, because she had decided to trust them.

Maybe said to Strawgirl as they drove through the forest, 'I hope Jimmy made it back before they woke, otherwise they would be suspicious. They'd wonder where he was in the middle of the night.'

'Yes,' said Strawgirl.

'I hope he was telling us the truth. I hope I've done the right thing.' Maybe took the four-wheel-drive Land Rover too fast round a bend and skidded a little.

'Yes,' Strawgirl said, quietly.

They jumped down from the Land Rover in the middle of the forest. They knew the brothers must come this way if Jimmy was telling the truth. Strawgirl looked at the pines. She worked out which tree was the oldest. Among trees, the oldest tree is always the leader. She flew to the top of the tallest tree's branches and whispered urgently into its foliage, then she landed down beside Maybe. 'Yes,' she said.

In a forest, trees are not individuals. They act like a community. They form part of a single organism. They breathe together. If one tree leans to the west, the next leans to the east. They know about each other's presence. If a stream flows to the south, the tree will lean to the north. If one tree's foliage grows mainly on the right, the other tree will grow mainly on the left, so that together their foliage can form an umbrella. Trees from the same family don't compete with each other. Maybe had loved her forest all her life. Without knowing anything about trees, she had sensed their harmony and their mystery. Now the unity of the trees was going to come in handy.

37

Irene's Surprise

It was nine o'clock in the evening, Wednesday night. Maybe was worked up to high doh. She never went to bed now before eleven o'clock. She and Irene were washing and drying the dishes, Maybe doing the washing, Irene doing the drying and putting away. Tonight was the night that the brothers were coming for more cows, according to Jimmy. Maybe was full of apprehension. Even with Jimmy on their side, she wasn't sure they were going to win.

Irene MacPherson had not yet told Maybe of the surprise she had planned for that night so when Maybe said to her, 'Were you just planning on giving up our home, our farm, without a fight?' she simply said, 'I'm tired.'

Maybe exploded. 'You're tired! What about me? I do everything. You just lie about the place.'

'Be quiet, Maybe!'

'Look, I've told you a hundred times. That man Jimmy has warned us himself. They are coming tonight. You know two of our cows are missing.

What are you going to do about it? Have you rung the police?'

'Yes.'

'And?'

'They are sceptical, put it that way, but they are coming tomorrow to pay a visit. They were tied up today.'

To anybody listening, it would have seemed as if Maybe was the adult and Irene the child. 'Oh, so you just accepted that!' Maybe snapped.

'Stop picking on me!' Irene said petulantly.

Maybe gave her a look. It was just as well that she had Jimmy on their side, when the men came tonight. She would need him.

'Look, I know I've not been the best mum in the world but I've been grieving.'

'I've been grieving too!' Maybe shouted. All the weeks of suppressed grief welled up and overflowed.

'People grieve in different ways,' Irene said. 'Some people do lots to keep themselves busy and hide from their feelings, and other people do nothing and are overcome by their feelings. There is no right or wrong.'

There was nothing Maybe could say to this, so she scowled instead. It was still infuriating to her the way her mother had just been lying about the place, doing nothing for weeks. Self-pity was silly as far as Maybe was concerned. She didn't like the girl at school who trailed around the building, weeping. But something nagged at Maybe: was it true that she had been too busy? Had she even been deliberately busy? There was no time to ask insane questions. 'Look, Mum,' she said, 'they are coming for four more cows tonight, TONIGHT, in about three hours' time, and what have you done about it? Nothing. Zilch.' She threw the wet cloth she was holding against the wall.

'I think you'll find I've been a bit busier than you think, if you just look out of the window about now,' Irene said, her voice trembling with emotion.

Maybe walked to the window and peered out. It was dark outside, but even so she could see them advancing; a group of people walking steadily along the track, all at one pace, as if they were of one mind. Like a herd of cows they stayed together, the neighbouring farmers and villagers – the Patons, the Airds, the Ineses, the Colqhouns, the MacIntoshes, the Cochranes, the Todds, the Haldanes armed with large pitchforks, and their children, allowed up late for this special night, armed with smaller pitchforks. There was the local Spar woman, Mrs MacKenzie; Fergus from the garage, the pub owners, Bob and Barbara McShine; Maybe's teacher – her teacher! – Ms Rose; and, to Maybe's utter and total and complete astonishment, Spider. Maybe was bowled over. There was a weak feeling in her knees, a dizzy feeling in her head, the sound of hope rushing fast between her ears. She had thought they'd have to slug this out on their own, just Strawgirl, herself and Jimmy. But now they had help. Now they had an army.

'Mum!' said Maybe. ' Oh, Mum! How? How did you do this?'

'I did it just sitting around doing nothing!' Irene said, not prepared to let the ball pass without kicking it in the goal.

Maybe hugged her mother. 'I'm sorry,' she said, tears pouring down her face.

'Me too,' said Irene. 'I did a ring around when I finally woke up. No way are we losing Wishing Well.'

Maybe jumped up and down. 'We have help! We are going to win!'

The herd of people had nearly reached the farmhouse. 'Now Maybe, this is your call. You do the talking. I'm not quite up to that yet,' Irene said, her arm round Maybe's shoulder.

Maybe stood on a soapbox inside her barn and addressed her friends and supporters. Ms Rose beamed with pride. Maybe told them all about the twin brothers, how they had been sending the Macphersons blackmail letters, how they had stolen two cows already, how they were planning on selling the land to a development company which was going to build a Domino supermarket. Tommy Haldane brought out a petition – it had one hundred signatures on it already! 'Anyone here who hasn't already signed this petition can sign it now,' he said. 'They can't build a supermarket slap bang in the middle of our village. It won't be allowed. They would have had to get planning permission, and permission from residents. These brothers have probably made the whole thing up to get you off the land. They are crooks. I know of somebody else who has had the dirty done by the Barnes-Gutteridge brothers. They are criminals.'

'Tonight, hopefully, we'll catch them red-handed and that will prove it!' Maybe said. She hoped against hope that Jimmy wouldn't change his mind and confess to the brothers that he'd spilled the beans. She hoped that they were still intending to come tonight. She hadn't heard a word from Jimmy since he left in the middle of the night, nearly twenty-four hours ago.

Maybe thanked everyone for coming to help. Tommy Haldane spoke for them all when he said, 'We are not just helping you, lass, we are helping ourselves.' Quite a few people said, 'Aye,' and clapped their hands, including, unexpectedly, Spider.

It was unnerving for Maybe to see her old foe at the farm, turned now into a supporter. Spider actually smiled back, which was even more bizarre. He came up to her and said, 'The others are too shy to come. They thought you wouldn't want them here.' Maybe looked at Spider closely. She couldn't bring herself to trust him yet, but nor could she ask him to leave. She would let him stay for now – see what happened.

It was ten o'clock at night. Tommy said that the children should all stay in the house and that the adults should be outside, some along the forest road, some hiding in the fields next to the cows. Maybe protested. 'I've been managing all of this on my own,' she said. 'I also know the forest best, and that's the way they will come. In an hour's time, I'll go there and wait. As soon as I see them coming, I'll send the signal.'

Tommy almost relented. 'You won't be fast enough, they'll be in a trailer,' he said.

'Yes, I will. I'll drive my Land Rover and hide it where they can't see it. Then I'll take the other road home through the forest, the one that runs more or less parallel to the one they will be taking.'

Maureen, Tommy's wife, piped up. 'This is Maybe's farm,' she said. 'I think you should be taking instructions from her. She's managed so far. Don't be coming here and taking over now!' she laughed, patting her husband on the back. 'He has a tendency to take over, haven't you, darling?' Tommy looked embarrassed.

'Right!' Maybe said, seizing the moment.

'I want to come with you,' Spider volunteered.

'Me too,' said Violet.

'And me!' said Ms Rose.

'Can you use me?' said Angus, who was so tall he looked like a grown man.

It was, to Maybe, the most incredible feeling, this camaraderie; it sent goose bumps up and down her arms and shivers down her back. Not the goose bumps you get when you are frightened, but the ones that come with intense appreciation and pleasure. At last, it felt as if Wishing Well Farm might remain her home.

Outside, the smoke from the kitchen fire billowed confidently into the darkness. If the smoke were able to write letters, it would spell H-O-M-E.

38

The Trees of the Forest

Everybody was nervous. It seemed that the heart of every person beat with exactly the same fierce rhythm. If their heartbeats could have been amplified, they would have sounded like African drums. There was a fresh excitement blowing in the wind. Maybe was so alert, her body was stiff. Her ears were as sharp as instinct. Her dark eyes gleamed brightly. She was defending her beloved cows.

Everyone carried a torch: Morag, from Maybe's class; Violet, her good friend; Ms Rose. Violet was so excited she looked like she might disintegrate. Maybe felt shy with Ms Rose. It was strange having her on her side with Maybe being the boss this time. Ms Rose was wearing jeans and a fleece and her hair was loose about her face. She looked completely different from how she looked in school. However, now was not the time to get seized by embarrassment: there was work to be done. Those twins were going to get the fright of their lives. Maybe remembered reading somewhere that surprise was the most important ingredient in winning a battle. Take the enemy by surprise. She felt like she was involved in a battle – the battle of Wishing Well Farm.

Violet, Ms Rose, Morag, Spider and big Angus climbed into the Land Rover. Maybe drove competently and quickly through the forest till she came to the top of a hill. She could see down but the men wouldn't be able to see up.

'I didn't know you could drive!' Spider said, astonished.

'My dad taught me,' Maybe said coolly, as if she had much more important things on her mind.

For some people, fear makes them talk nineteen to the dozen and shriek with hysteria at the slightest sound or movement. For others, fear dries them up, makes them still and silent and stiff. Violet, Angus and Morag were in the former category. Spider, Ms Rose and Maybe were in the latter. 'They're coming. I think I see them!' Morag shrieked. 'Look! What's that?'

'What?' Maybe whispered, on her feet at once.

'There!' Morag screamed, pointing at nothing.

'I've seen something!' Angus shouted. And once again, Morag and Violet violently trembled and shook in the car, while Maybe, Spider and Ms Rose kept perfectly still.

'Calm down!' Maybe ordered. 'Conserve your energy for the enemy.'

Maybe and her team were on the low forest road. Maybe had parked the Land Rover behind a tree. They wouldn't be seen there. As soon as they spotted the trailer coming, they could take off along the low road and get back to the farm quickly. Strawgirl was already in position, high up in a pine tree. Maybe hoped against hope that Jimmy had been telling the truth and that the twins would be approaching the farm from the back road in their trailer. Her whole strategy depended on this. But what if he was a liar? What if this was the most cunning device of all – a sophisticated booby trap? Suddenly Maybe was not so sure any more. She doubted her tactics. She doubted Jimmy's motives. She looked anxiously towards the farmhouse in case the men were going to approach from the front after all. Yes, she had her women and men there, but they wouldn't have any warning.

At this very minute, most of the villagers were in the farmhouse staying warm, while Tommy Haldane was keeping watch for the signal, the flashing-light code, that Maybe would start. Alec Todd, Barbara McShine, Hugh Paton, Lesley Colqhoun, Charlie MacIntosh and Peter Aird were all positioned on the forest low road at various intervals waiting to receive Maybe's signal and pass it on back to the house. Flash, flash, flash from relay to relay. It meant: HERE THEY COME. One of the downsides about having such a large farm with so many acres was that it took quite some time, even by car, to get from one bit to another.

Strawgirl was right at the top of a tree; no one but Maybe knew she was there. And anyway, Maybe remembered with a dull feeling across her chest, no one could see Strawgirl except herself.

Suddenly, Maybe looked up at Strawgirl who, to her astonishment, was gesticulating wildly and pointing. Right enough, the men were coming. They were coming all right.

The trailer crawled along the forest road. It looked like a predator, snaking its way round the bends of the road. There was no time now for Maybe to feel frightened or nervous. She sprang into action, flashing her torch at Peter Aird who was 400 metres away in the darkness. She saw Peter's bright little message flash through the darkness to Charlie MacIntosh, from Charlie MacIntosh to Lesley Colquhoun. Strawgirl was up above, whispering frantically to the trees. Maybe jumped into her Land Rover and started driving as fast as she could up the road back to the farmhouse. Ms Rose had to hang on to the side of the vehicle for dear life.

And then something odd happened. A large shape moved up the slope and on to the high forest road. 'Wow!' Spider shouted, peering through the window into the darkness. 'Something big is moving out there!'

'What's going on?' Morag screamed.

Maybe stared up the road. It appeared the very trees were moving. No, that couldn't be right. The trees had never moved in the whole of Maybe's life.

This was one of those occasions when Maybe literally could not believe her eyes.

Strawgirl! It had to be Strawgirl!

39

The Brave Wooden Soldiers

'What is going on!' Arnold said, in a tight, breathless voice as the pine trees started to move. It could be a trick of the light; maybe he was hallucinating – but those trees looked like they were moving. They swayed from side to side, then walked. Some now stood right outside his windscreen. They bent over so that he could no longer see out of his window; the entire windscreen was covered with tree, feathery needles pressed against the glass. More trees stood to the left and the right of the trailer, jammed right up against the body of the vehicle, and some trees stood at the back. Arnold could not drive forwards. He tried opening the driver's door. It would only move an inch or so; the trees were standing too close. They were trapped by trees!

Harold was in a panic. He hated being trapped anywhere – a toilet, a lift, the living room of his mother's house – let alone in the thickest of forests in the dead of night.

Jimmy was angry. This was not part of the plan.

The brothers should have been caught stealing the cows. This might frighten them off. The MacPhersons might never get the proof they needed.

'I knew there was something odd about that girl,' Harold said, practically hyperventilating. 'Anyone who can escape from a locked dungeon has to be strange, very strange.' He looked at Jimmy. 'This is your fault!'

'Why is it my fault?' Jimmy asked aggressively.

'It just is,' Harold said.

'That little girl is a witch,' Arnold said.

Suddenly, Harold had a fine idea. His newspaper was lying in the front of the trailer. He rolled it into thin tubes – the kind you make to start a fire – then he pulled his lighter out from his jacket pocket and lit a couple of papers.

'If we throw these out of the window, they are bound to make the trees move back. Forest fire spreads fast. With a bit of luck, we can burn the whole forest down. It will be a job well done anyway because we would have needed to get rid of the trees for the supermarket.' Harold laughed.

'Dinny do that!' Jimmy shouted, but it was too late. Harold chucked some papers out quickly; the fire was rapidly moving down to his fingers. Outside the window, the flames sizzled for a minute and then went out. He lit a couple more papers, allowing them dangerously to catch into wild flames in his hands before he threw them out of the window. This time the fire caught alarmingly quickly. It ran along the floor of the forest and licked the base of the pine trees. A ferocious orange, a frantic yellow, a fiery red whipped the trees, spitting and crackling, dancing a frenetic fire-wind jig. The pine trees were fighting for their lives. Some backed away from the trailer towards the farmhouse where it was safe. They looked like a whole army retreating, over one hill and down another, marching, their branches swaying like soldiers' arms. Side to side: one, two, three, four. One, two, three, four.

Maybe looked back. She couldn't believe her bad luck. The forest was on fire behind her. She would have to go back and save Strawgirl. She knew Strawgirl couldn't cope with fire. It had all gone wrong. Strawgirl was not supposed to have made the trees move! Why had she done that? It was crazy.

'What's happening?' Ms Rose shouted.

'Can you drive?' Maybe asked Ms Rose.

'Yes,' Ms Rose said.

'Well, drive back to the farmhouse. Keep going straight along this road till you come to a fork. Take the left path – that will lead you to the farm. Tell them to go ahead without me. I've got to go back and put out this fire.'

'You can't. Not on your own!' Ms Rose said, horrified.

'I'll go with her,' Spider said.

'No,' said Maybe. 'I have to go on my own. I'll be

fine. I know the forest like the back of my hand. Go now. Hurry!'

Fire was the only adversary that Strawgirl could not fight. Maybe knew that fire had always petrified her friend. Once, in the farmhouse when Maybe had lit a fire in the hearth, Strawgirl had screamed. Even the sound of a fire scared her half to death: the crackle and spit, the snaps and splints, the swearing, the cursing, the shattering and breaking of brittle bones. 'Fire!' Strawgirl had sobbed to Maybe. 'Fire, angry!'

Maybe ran now to where Strawgirl was standing, shaking, staring at the forest fire in horror. It was catching, it was spreading, faster than disease or belief or vicious gossip. The trees that had blocked the trailer had all backed off. The vehicle was now driving forwards, towards the farmhouse; the men would go for the cows now.

As Maybe stood watching the wild raging beast of the fire streaking and stretching its hot claws through the forest, she felt totally defeated, at the mercy of the murderous flames. Why fight for Wishing Well Farm only for the forest to burn down? Maybe was hot. The smoke was pouring into her lungs. She coughed and spluttered. There was absolutely nothing she could do.

'Why did you make the trees move?' she asked Strawgirl, exasperated.

'Can't help,' Strawgirl said. 'Nature.' Maybe didn't quite understand what she meant. Did she mean she couldn't help herself? Did she mean it was part of her own nature to fight in this way? That when she saw the trailer approaching, she had to use her powers, but couldn't control them? There was no time to work it out.

'Gone wrong,' Strawgirl said, sadly. Maybe stood, in horror, staring at her burning trees.

Strawgirl saw that Maybe was angry with her and was galvanized into action. 'NO!' she screamed. She could not let Maybe down. She had to do something. She knew she couldn't defeat the fire alone. Then, all of a sudden, she had a frightening idea.

Up ahead, the surviving trees were hurrying for their lives as the forest fire raged on. Strawgirl made the hardest decision she had ever had to make. She called thirty of them back. The trees marched towards her, retracing the ground, walking back into danger. 'Sorry,' she said. 'Back.' She pointed a trembling straw finger down the hill towards the fire. 'Back, back, back.'

It was only the second time Maybe had seen Strawgirl cry. She understood that Strawgirl wanted the trees to give their lives to save other trees. 'Be brave, trees,' Maybe told them, hugging one of them quickly. 'You'll die knowing you have saved your forest and your farm. We will plant more of you in your memory.' Maybe was trying not to cry. She felt as if she had aged about ten years in the past few weeks.

One by one, the fine, tall pine trees bravely marched down the hill. One by one they approached their deaths, calmly and with a dignity that made

Maybe tremble. She stood watching the whole scene with her eyes wide open. The first tree fell on the fire; then a second tree fell. It made no difference. The fire raged on. Strawgirl flew back down, as near to the fire as she could get without endangering her life. It was so intensely hot, the very air was burning and smouldering. 'Together! Now!' she ordered. And a huge group of trees fell down. All of them. All at once. It was an incredible thing to witness. The trees flattened the fire. Strawgirl took one last look at the awful sight of it – thirty trees, burned out and blackened by a fire, all dead, some hollow, and every root dead and lifeless. Branches broken and black lay strewn everywhere as if the trees had exploded.

Strawgirl flew back to Maybe and stood solemnly beside her. Maybe bowed her head over the carcasses of the trees and vowed they would not be forgotten. Strawgirl bowed her head too. Then Maybe and Strawgirl took flight, up into the charcoal clouds, through the hot smouldering air and back to the farmhouse. They landed behind the building, out of sight. The night air smelled of battle. Maybe was never going to forget this night as long as she lived.

40

The Battle of the Braes

Harold and Arnold opened the back door of the trailer and let down the ramp. Harold grabbed the bag with the injection needles and the sedative. He was in a terrible hurry; the sooner they got the job done and got back to Cull, the better. This whole place was terrifying. There was something strange about the land, about the trees, even about the moonlight. It cast a particularly eerie light over the fields. It looked to him as if the entire place was caught under a spell. Harold was not a fanciful man. He did not believe in spirits or ghosts or poltergeists or anything to do with the supernatural. He didn't believe in God. Up until tonight he had believed in what he could see, in the quotidian – the everyday. But tonight, Harold couldn't swear to what he had seen. He wasn't sure what had happened.

There was no time to think about it. They had to get the job done and get back. It was still dark. Nobody was about, thankfully. Harold would not shed any tears over this place being brought down, that was for sure.

Jimmy jumped out of the trailer too. It was his job to talk to the cows. He wondered if the girl had taken him seriously, if she had managed to warn her mother that they would be coming. There was no sign anywhere of any extra cars or any police. He hoped for her sake that she had.

Jimmy, Harold and Arnold opened the gate and went through the first field and into the second, where the cows were standing huddled together in one large group, watching the familiar strangers approach under the spooky moonlight.

Jimmy walked slowly, talking softly to the cows, as he had planned with Molly. He would encourage the twins to steal the cows, and then she would catch the brothers red-handed and call the police. Jimmy advised her to get the brothers tied up. 'I don't understand how you got me trussed up in that rope, but do it again to them,' he'd said. Harold and Arnold walked behind him. Harold had a long rope in his hand. They would get the halter round the neck of a cow and drag it to the trailer. One cow stood alone, away from the mass of cows. Jimmy walked towards that one. Harold threw the rope round its neck.

All at once, it seemed, and in one startling movement, people appeared from everywhere, from behind the trees, from behind the fence, from the ditches, from the ridges of ploughed land. They all shone their torches and lamps in the dark. 'Stop!' one man shouted. 'We've got you!'

Of course, in any kind of trouble it is a person's instinct to run first and think later. This was just what Harold and Arnold did. They didn't notice that Jimmy stood quite still. Tommy Haldane and Charlie MacIntosh jumped on him. Maybe intervened. 'Leave him. He's on our side.'

It was Spider who couldn't wait any longer. Desperate to prove himself to Maybe, he picked up a large stone and hurled it as far as he could in the direction of the escaping twins. From the top of a sycamore tree, Strawgirl helped the stone along, so that it seemed to the eyes of the watching children that it flew in the air for the most incredible arc of time until it landed smack bang on Arnold's head and knocked him down. Spider was astonished at the distance the stone had travelled, but then he had been doing weights recently and his muscles were rock solid. In seconds, Arnold was on his feet again, rubbing his head and running towards his twin.

Then all hell was let loose. Maybe's men and women rushed for the twins, their pitchforks raised. There were shouts and cries for blood. Maybe intervened again. 'We don't want violence!' she shouted. 'We want justice. We want our land. Catch them and bring them to the farmhouse. Mum! Call the police!'

But the cows didn't understand Maybe's wise words. They recognized the twins as the men who had come and stolen two of their kind in the dead of night. Cows never forget an enemy. They came charging down the field towards the men, galloping in a straight line with their heads down. Ten cows came from one side and ten from another till they encircled the twins completely. They started to close in on them until all that could be seen were the brothers' heads and their terrified eyes.

The twins had difficulty breathing; the cows were so close. They pushed against Harold and Arnold until they fell down. Maybe was horrified. The cows were about to trample the twins to death. 'Strawgirl!' Maybe shouted. 'Stop this! Get them to move back!' Her friends eyed her curiously. Who was she talking to? they wondered.

Instantly, the cows parted and the circle was broken. They moved back, slowly, reluctantly, then wandered off at an easy pace, swaying their behinds back and forth in the night. They almost looked stylish. The twins were not badly hurt, just a bit bruised, but they were absolutely terrified. It had to have been the most horrifying experience of their twin lives. The wary men got to their feet and hobbled tentatively, meekly, in the direction of Maybe.

They would go into the kitchen. They would give themselves up to the police. It was better than being trampled to death by a herd of cows, any day.

All of the children ran after them, screaming and laughing. They'd never had so much fun. The police car arrived, its light flashing in the dark. An hour later the car left with the twin brothers inside. Apparently, the Inland Revenue wanted the brothers; they were investigating a massive tax evasion. The twins were also wanted for questioning for their handling of two large business enterprises and on several counts of fraud. What with one thing and another, the stealing of cows and the illegal transport of animals, the cooking of their accounts books and their shady deals on various business ventures, the brothers could be looking at twenty years each, courtesy of Her Majesty's prison. It was the purest moment of triumph: Wishing Well Farm, at last free from threats. To celebrate, the children danced the dance of the pitchforks under the full moonlight.

It was the latest any of them had ever been allowed up apart from New Year. They laid their pitchforks across the ground like Highland swords and danced over them. Angus and Violet pretended they were the instruments, humming a Highland jig that became faster and faster until they all fell on the ground, giggling and exhausted. Most of them would sleep through the following day, and Maybe's class would be much depleted. A drained Ms Rose would stand in front of the blackboard trying to remember what she had just said.

The danger was over; the twins had been arrested. In Jimmy the farm would gain a new and trusty farmhand. Everyone was still celebrating and dancing when Maybe and Strawgirl sneaked off. They had work to do. Madame Bovary and Memphis Minnie were still abandoned at the abattoir. Maybe realized that something had to be done to get them back, not tomorrow or the next day, but tonight, before the shady guy at the abattoir ordered their slaughter.

41

Memphis and Madame

It was time to face the cold night air swirling over the abattoir. Maybe shivered just thinking about the place. She hoped Strawgirl would remember the way. Maybe had not yet been there. The whole idea of the place gave her the creeps, it really did. The total creeps. It was a place that served no purpose whatsoever other than to illegally kill cattle – to slaughter them and skin them and chop them into slices.

And so the two of them went out into the blue night with the stars firmly pinned in the sky. Maybe flew so confidently at Strawgirl's side that you would think she had never heard of vertigo. It made Strawgirl laugh to look to the right and see that not only could Maybe fly high in the night sky, but that Maybe's flying was really quite dynamic. She dipped and turned and floated and streaked with her arms out and her body straight; she looked like a truly glorious thing, a fabulous girl with wings. It made Strawgirl laugh. If only Maybe could still do this without her; if only it were possible to leave her powers behind, like some people leave treasured possessions for close friends and family. If only Strawgirl could put her powers in a special box with a red velvet lid. Maybe could open it thinking it was a new jewellery box, to discover a tiny phial with a bright liquid in it and a lovely note from Strawgirl in typically scratchy handwriting: *My powers, girl, I leave them*. Wouldn't that just be so good?

Strawgirl was fantasizing about this as she flew through the sky with Maybe at her side. It was a longer flight than she remembered.

Suddenly, she noticed the trees looming down below, the big rock directly beneath them. It was time to begin descent. 'Good luck, Strawgirl!' Maybe shouted as she flew down, down, right through the last low-lying cloud and into the tops of the trees, and down again to the top of the abattoir's gate.

They went on foot from there, along a dark path, until they came to the huge metal doors. They were locked, of course. Strawgirl used a piece of her straw to unpick the lock. There, inside the cold stone abattoir, were Madame Bovary and Memphis Minnie standing alone. There were no other cattle with them. They had been sleeping standing up. They looked, in the dim light, like strange beasts from another world. Their pink tongues hung out at the side of their mouths. Their legs were impossibly thin. Their big eyes drooped. But worst of all, the skin that usually fitted so tightly around their bodies was loose, horrifyingly loose, flapping at their sides like so much extra leather. Clearly these cows had not been fed since they'd got here. They were very nearly dead.

Maybe stared at her cows in disbelief. Their eyes were blank and they did not seem to recognize her at all. Maybe filled her hands with water from the outside tap and poured it into Madame Bovary's mouth. A slow tongue lolled around a little and licked a drop. Maybe did the same again, this time rubbing the outside of Madame Bovary's mouth with her own fingers. Not only were they starving, the poor creatures, but they were also terribly thirsty. It was clear from their glassy eyed stares that the cows were dehydrated.

'We have to get them home then call the vet, or they will die,' Maybe sobbed.

Strawgirl agreed. She stood in the corner of the barn, trying to pull herself together, to summon the last bit of energy and magic she would need to use in her straw life to get the cows home. For her, it was the last hundred feet in the climb up the mountain, the last lap in the long race. It was that terrible moment when you really do not think you can make it. The moment that always occurs seconds before you are about to give up. Strawgirl wanted to crawl not walk, to sleep not fly, to give in, to give up, and to say finally, enough, enough. She looked at Maybe and saw something on her face that she had never seen before: belief. Maybe was standing, there totally confident that Strawgirl could pull this off, that she could get those cows home. Maybe hadn't doubted her for a second. Strawgirl couldn't let Maybe down.

Strawgirl led the cows outside, till they were all standing in the country road. She took a deep breath; her straw flushed pink, like strawberry-blonde hair, with the enormous effort of it all. Breathe in, then out. The noise she made was like the wind's high whistle. Maybe had never heard it before. Strawgirl stretched out her arms. Like a conductor, she waved her arm at Maybe first, who rose effortlessly into the air, then at Madame Bovary, who also rose up and up, her hooves shining like stars in the sky, her white chest and piebald face moving in and out of the clouds. Then it was Memphis's turn. Her legs struggled and flailed, her body was at right angles to the earth. She moved so slowly she looked like she wasn't moving at all. Strawgirl took another deep breath – breathe in, then out – desperate to save both cows. Strawgirl squeezed her fingers together and furrowed her forehead in tight concentration. It was now or it was never. One, two, three.

And suddenly, Memphis was moving, up and up and gloriously up, her black-and-white body roaring through the sky, past the Plough and Orion and the brightest planet of all, Venus. Memphis Minnie was on the move. She was on her way home. Strawgirl lifted herself up and flew alongside Maybe, Memphis and Madame Bovary, and she never saw a more fabulous sight than when Memphis jumped over the moon. Way down below, a little dog barked.

42

Winter

Maybe thought that winter was Strawgirl's least favourite season. Her hair had icicles in it and her face looked brittle and pinched. Clouds of icy winter breath came out of her mouth when she spoke. She felt damp when Maybe hugged her.

Snow didn't melt on Strawgirl; it just stayed there till she shook it off in a flurry of powdery white. Strawgirl shivered and blew about in the bitter wind. It grew dark early and Strawgirl would hide in the barn to try and keep warm. The trees were bare and stark against the sky, suddenly alone. They looked noble in the winter, as if they had found themselves ill all at once and were waiting patiently to get better. The woods were dark and serious and sombre like people at a funeral. Strawgirl's black silhouette was outlined against the gloomy winter sky.

Strawgirl was heavier in the winter. She did not leap about or fly quickly through the air. Her very straw seemed to drag. All she wanted to do was sleep, keep warm, curl herself up into a ball of straw in the many, many hours of darkness.

Maybe wanted to make a snow girl when it snowed, but Strawgirl wasn't interested. The snow made her hands burn with cold. When the snow girl was finished Strawgirl stared at her jealously from the barn. She did look very silly with a carrot for her nose and coal for her eyes and buttons going all the way down her big fat belly, but all the same Maybe seemed very happy with the snow girl.

The winter earth was frozen; some plants did not survive the coldest season of all. The winter corn stayed under the ground in some fields, but most of the land lay fallow. Winter: the time when the sun reaches the south tropic, the tropic of Capricorn. The only lively, bright things that Strawgirl could see in the winter were the berries on the trees and bushes. A bright blood-red berry on the rowan trees.

43

In Ms Rose's Classroom

The school playground was covered in a thin frost like icing sugar sprinkled all over. Some parts of the playground were so icy you could skate across them. The railings were freezing cold in your hands. To the great annoyance of the pupils, salt had been thrown on some of the very slippery parts. Maybe was all wrapped up for the winter's day. She wore a tartan scarf around her neck, her thick grey dufflecoat and her navy-blue gloves. Her mother had insisted that she wear a vest under her school shirt today because the temperature was two degrees below freezing. Maybe was worried about Strawgirl, who loathed the cold.

In the classroom, Ms Rose was teaching a lesson on people and their differences. Maybe could tell the lesson was probably just for her. Ms Rose was not too subtle. 'Which ways are people different?' she asked the class.

'Colour,' said Maybe, before any one else said it.

'Religion,' said Violet.

'Some are fat, some are thin,' said Spider.

'Some are wealthy, some are poor,' said Troy. 'And some belong to a tribe,' he added.

Ms Rose looked at him closely. She didn't think he was being provocative. 'Which native people do we know about?' she asked the class.

'The Aborigines,' said Morag.

'The Maoris,' said Angus.

'Ibo,' said Maybe. 'My dad was an Ibo. I'm an Ibo really because he was one.'

'What do you know about the Ibo?' Ms Rose said.

'They are supposed to be honest, reliable, clever, small in height, dependable, good with money . . . a whole load of good things. My dad never told me anything bad about the Ibo, but then he was being like Scottish people are about themselves – proud.' Maybe laughed confidently.

Troy looked at her. Molly MacPherson was something, he thought. A look crossed his face. Ms Rose saw it. It was respect. He was listening to Maybe and looking at her with something akin to admiration in his eyes.

It seemed a whole lifetime ago that Maybe had felt embarrassed or ashamed about who she was. She would never again be ashamed to stand up in her class and say, 'My dad was an Ibo, and that makes me Ibo too,' she added proudly.

Maybe left school that day and went out into the playground. She looked up at the sky. The winter sun shone. It was as if her father had kept his promise, after all. She knew none of the bullies would ever bother her again.

44

Spring

In spring, Strawgirl's straw was much greener and her limbs squeaked when she moved, like grass blades when you whistle through them. Her straw hair was tousled with snowdrops and crocuses, narcissi and daffodils, and her eyes shone brightly like hard, young acorns. She loved the showery rain that blew in on the fresh winds, skipping and tumbling in it till her straw darkened and gleamed. She sniffed ferociously at her new spring, straw smell.

Strawgirl was full of surprises. One day, a frog hopped out of her lap and landed in Maybe's. When Maybe screamed, Strawgirl rolled away into a ball across the farmyard, shrieking with laughter. Another time, Maybe noticed a strange movement on Strawgirl's shoulder. A small nest was hidden there and, as Maybe stared in amazement, she saw that a tiny beak was pecking its way through a perfect pale-blue egg. Strawgirl just shrugged and said it itched.

In the springtime, Strawgirl's voice was different every day. She gossiped with a lamb's bleat or laughed

like a cuckoo. She scattered herself on the wind and
landed in a heap at Maybe's feet as three baby rabbits
jumped out of her chest.

45

Cleaning Up

The time for the Harvest Dance had come round again and Maybe was excitedly cleaning the barn for the big night. Not her favourite job, but she had reasons to be cheerful. The illegal abattoir had been shut down. The brothers were in prison pending a trial. As well as being tried for their illegal business ventures, the brothers faced an arson charge for setting Maybe's forest alight. Maybe reflected on her own glory and swept the barn as Strawgirl slept on top of a tall pile of bales.

Lately, Strawgirl had been awfully sleepy. Her straw was in a bit of a mess, as if she was half coming apart. Her eyes were dull and not nearly so lively as usual. 'Soon gone,' she said once, but Maybe didn't understand. What was it that made Maybe notice these things? It was odd – afterwards she remembered everything the way people do remember everything after a really big event. Yet, at the time, she didn't know the big event was coming. How was that? How did it happen? Perhaps we all live ahead of ourselves in some way, in order to turn round and look back. Right now there was no time to wonder what was happening to Strawgirl. Perhaps it was just exhaustion. Perhaps she felt deflated now that the farm was safe – that feeling you get when you look forward to something for ages, then it happens, then it is over. The air comes out of you; you sag. Call it the Boxing Day syndrome. A good night's sleep would cure Strawgirl – or so Maybe hoped.

Maybe cleaned six months' worth of cow dung out of the dark barn without so much as a moan or a groan. She sang to herself as she swept. All of a sudden, it seemed life might just get bearable. Not a girl to rush for exaggerations, Maybe might, at a stretch have called herself 'happy'. It was a wonderful feeling. When she was a very small girl, she had taken happiness for granted. Now, Maybe felt as if she had grown up. She understood the price you could pay for happiness. In the hardest possible way, she had learned that you could be happy one minute and, in a snap of the fingers, have that happiness snatched from under your very eyes. Life could change. Just like that.

So Maybe swept the barn and counted her blessings. She had a mother who loved her and who was beautiful and who smelled nicer than anybody else's mother did. She had a farm with wonderful cows and fields that were rich with corn and hay and crops. She had a good harvest this year, starting in July and finishing at the end of August; good straw, excellent grain. She had friends at school who admired her. Some of her friends, Maybe thought to herself, smiling, were actually 'in awe' of her. But best of all, and to the best of her knowledge, Maybe MacPherson was the only girl in the whole of the Highlands who had her very own real, live Strawgirl.

Strawgirl lay with her straw arms curled around her head. Maybe could see the hot steam of Strawgirl's breath. She could hear her snoring; there seemed lots of *sssssssszzzzzttts* on the way out of her mouth and lots of *aaaaaaaahhhs* on the way in. Maybe listened, fascinated, for a few moments, wondering if Strawgirl's sleep was alphabetical in some way.

It was the first time she had actually looked forward to something for a long time. It was exactly a year since her father had died, because this time last year they were cleaning the barn for the dance. Maybe went out of the barn towards her kitchen to get a drink. She stopped at the old wishing well and threw in a coin. The first wish was for her dad. 'I wish my dad could see the barn dance,' she whispered to herself. It must be possible to see things from heaven, with the sky as your eyes. Maybe didn't believe in God properly but she did believe in heaven. She liked the idea of there being a heaven somewhere housing her dad. The second wish was for Strawgirl. 'I wish Strawgirl could live forever,' Maybe whispered with her eyes shut, clenching her fists.

In the kitchen, her mother looked tired again, as

if all the recent activity had drained the blood from her. Actually, her mum didn't look tired so much as sad. 'Are you thinking of Dad?' Maybe asked her.

Irene was surprised. How strange it was to have a daughter who always knew your mind, who could read your thoughts and feelings, who could even tell what you were feeling before you knew yourself. As far as Irene was concerned, she had been bright and breezy, but she couldn't fool Maybe. 'Yes,' she said, frankly. 'It is a year to the day. Anniversaries are horrible. It would be nice if, at least for the first year, the calendar just skipped a day out of respect for my feelings.'

Maybe laughed. 'Do you ever see him?' she said, braving it.

'Your father?'

'Yes.' Maybe was a little breathless. 'Because I see him sometimes. I've caught glimpses of him bending down in the dairy, and once I saw him at the end of the far field, running ahead of me.'

'That's nice,' Irene said.

'It's not nice,' Maybe said. 'It's really strange. He's not real.'

'In a way he is real,' Irene said, cheering up considerably. 'Think how pleased your dad would be if he knew you'd caught glimpses of him. He'd know it was your mind playing tricks, but he'd like that. He'd like the fact that he was still in your mind.'

'Of course he's in my mind! I'll never forget him!'

'Well, there you are. If you never forget him, you won't ever lose him. Don't worry about it,' Irene said.

'But we have lost him,' Maybe said, impatiently.

'Well, yes, we have, but not completely. We can still keep him alive in our minds. We can still talk to him and see his face and wave to him and whatever we like. We can still plant his favourite flowers and play his favourite music. You could still sing that song he was teaching you for your party piece at the barn dance last year.' Irene was crying as she said all this.

'If we can still do all this why are you crying?' Maybe asked, suddenly sad herself, beyond words.

'Because I miss him too,' Irene said, crying more. 'He was a lovely, lovely man, your father. A big, special man.' Irene walked away to the fridge and poured herself a drink. 'Let's have some fresh orange juice and then go and finish the barn together.' They both wiped the tears away with the backs of their hands.

In the barn, Irene helped Maybe to put up the streamers, to hang big, bright bunches of balloons from the beams, to make a small stage from old wooden boxes turned upside down, to put the bales down to be used as chairs.

'It is past five,' Irene said startled. 'I think we've done enough for today.'

'You go on in then, and I'll just finish this off,' Maybe said.

When Irene had gone, Maybe climbed up to the top of the bales to find Strawgirl. She was still fast asleep. Maybe decided not to disturb her. She kissed her straw cheek and whispered, 'I love you, Strawgirl' into her friend's ear.

Strawgirl stirred a little. 'Me too,' she mumbled and slipped back to sleep.

46

Harvest Moon

On the night of the barn dance, a huge harvest moon gleamed from the glittering night sky. Maybe beamed up at it. It was as if the sky had heard about her dance and was all dressed up for the ball. There were the silver stars in their dark gowns, sparkling brightly. There were the clouds with their long skirts trailing across the sky. There was the moon, the most beautiful belle of the ball, up there with a bright orange glow all the way round it, like the wonderful orange hem of a skirt. There was the sky itself, a deep, dazzling, dark blue.

Maybe could hardly believe her luck, a full moon for her harvest dance.

It was a terrible pity that Strawgirl was still feeling a little poorly, but Maybe didn't have time to worry about that. Strawgirl was quite comfortable up on her bale of hay where she could watch the whole wonderful dance take place. All of Maybe's battle friends turned up for the barn dance: Violet, Morag and Angus. Spider was wearing a great pair of silver trousers with about twenty pockets all over them. Troy and Moron had asked if they could come, and Maybe had said 'yes'. Moron turned up wearing a checked shirt that just about fitted him. Troy hadn't yet arrived. All of the adults from the neighbouring farms were there, dressed up too.

The band played Scottish folk music, for the ceilidh had begun in earnest, and it was almost as if the fiddle players were competing to see who could play the fastest. In the local band, Slanjiva, there were two fiddle players, one drummer, and one woman with long black hair who played the harmonica. Already people were dancing. 'Hooch! Hooch!' they shouted, spinning around on each other's arms. Dancing made everyone light-headed and happy. There was no tomorrow, just this minute now, to spin and shake, backwards and forwards. Such a wonderful feeling of camaraderie, of friendship, dancing in figures of eight, exchanging a friend's arm for a stranger's. Maybe loved the moment when you looked straight into your partner's eyes and then passed on to the next partner and looked into their eyes. It was as if there was an invisible spirit being passed on from person to person. Strange, to suddenly find herself holding Spider's hand. His face was flushed red. Mostly everybody was dancing. It was the kind of atmosphere where everybody wanted to join in and hurl themselves around in circles until they made themselves hysterical and dizzy. The adults didn't seem to get dizzy dancing though. Maybe couldn't work that out.

The food was laid out on a long trestle table. The adults drank beer and whisky. The children drank apple juice and Coke. There were sausage rolls, chicken drumsticks, sandwiches, crisps and several of her mum's wonderful home-made cakes. A Victoria sponge, a gingerbread, a fruit loaf, butterfly cakes and rock cakes. It was the first time Irene had baked in a long time.

It was time to do 'Strip the Willow'. They formed two long lines with Fred, who shouted instructions at everybody and shook his head in frustration. 'How difficult *is* this?' he shouted. 'Come on, make a bridge.' Irene was standing at the side in her beautiful blue dress that Jamie had loved. She looked magnificent.

Maybe went up to her and said, 'May I have this dance?' Irene laughed and took her daughter's hand, and they charged up and down the long aisle, laughing. At the end of 'Strip the Willow', Maybe was completely out of breath. She kissed her mum on the cheek and said, 'Thank you,' and took a bow. Irene laughed. Maybe felt as if she had got her mother back, finally, properly. It was the first hearty laugh she had heard in a year.

Even the hens seemed to be enjoying the barn dance, clucking away to the twang of the fiddle. Some small children had already fallen asleep on the bales like fairy-tale children asleep on a bed of hay. The hay was steamy and warm. Maybe was ready to dance another dance in a figure of eight. She looked up at Strawgirl, beaming with pride. Her harvest dance was going brilliantly. Strawgirl waved back at her. Maybe did not realize it yet, but Strawgirl was saying goodbye.

Troy arrived when the dance was already in full swing, with his cousin, Hayley. Troy was wearing a kilt. He introduced Maybe to his cousin. 'This is Hayley. This is Molly.' he said. Hayley was wearing a brand-new red kilt. The two girls looked into each other's eyes; they knew at that very instant that they were going to be best friends. Their whole friend-future shone before them like a trusty star.

Maybe said, 'What is your second name? Is it the same as Troy's?'

'No, it's not,' Hayley said, 'because we are cousins through our mothers.'

'My name is Molly Siobhan MacPherson,' Maybe said. She liked old-fashioned introductions. She stared into Hayley's eyes. They were a bright blue-green. Something in their steady gaze reminded Maybe of somebody. She couldn't think for the moment who.

Hayley said, 'My full name is Hayley Rebecca Paterson.'

Maybe gasped and turned to where Strawgirl had been lying at the top of the bales of hay. Strawgirl was gone!

Fred proposed a toast. Everybody filled their

glasses with wine or beer or Irn-bru. Fred held his glass in their air. 'To absent friends,' he said.

Everybody said, 'Absent friends!' and chinked their glass with their neighbours.

Maybe chinked Hayley's glass. 'Absent friends,' she said again.

Hayley giggled and said, 'You make me laugh.'

Ms Rose came up to Maybe, holding a red kilt. 'I found this under a pile of hay,' she said. Ms Rose smiled at Maybe as if she had once, long ago, had her very own straw girl. Maybe took the kilt and hugged it, crying.

Fred was shouting over the microphone for Maybe to come and sing her song. Maybe walked the length of the barn till she came to the makeshift stage. Irene was watching her, smiling, thinking to herself, That girl of mine is tall now, so tall. Maybe took the microphone in her hand and started singing her father's Ibo song:

'Leave your hoes and dance with me. Titi chom
Leave your hoes and dance with me. Titi chom
You have come to do the lion's work. Titi chom
Now it's time to enjoy yourselves. Titi chom.'

Not only did Maybe sing the Ibo song, but she also danced an Ibo dance her father had taught her when she was a little girl. She found as she danced and moved her hips that her whole body liked doing the African dance, as if it had known the dance long before she did.

Irene wiped the tears from her eyes. The whole barn cheered. Ms Rose clapped loudly, her eyes filling too. She knew she wasn't supposed to have favourites, but Molly *was* her favourite. Maybe looked straight at her. As she sang, she could hear her father's voice just behind hers, singing along. It was a deep, mellow voice and she remembered the sound of it exactly. When Maybe stepped off the stage, her neighbours clapped her on the back.

'That was a lovely song, darling,' Isabel Aird said to her.

'Lovely,' said Margaret Haldane.

Maybe's cheeks were hot with pride. She knew she had sung her song well; she could feel it as she was doing it, as the song rose and flew like a bird from her mouth. How far it had travelled, her father's song.

Maybe looked around her, amazed to see that everyone was still clapping and cheering her. Out of the crowd came her new friend, Hayley Rebecca Paterson, with her corn-coloured hair. 'Would you like to dance with me, Molly MacPherson?' Hayley asked her.

'Certainly!' Maybe replied. The two of them danced a wild circle of eight to the left, to the right, to the left. Maybe looked up to the spot where Strawgirl had been. She remembered her saying, 'Soon gone.'

Maybe would never forget Strawgirl. How could she? She danced and danced with a lump in her throat and with her heart soaring and flying. It seemed strange to her that she could feel two emotions simultaneously: happiness and sadness. She was Molly Siobhan MacPherson of Wishing Well Farm, Grumbeg, and she had a brand-new best friend. But something about Hayley was so familiar.

Ms Rose came up to Maybe. 'That was a wonderful Ibo song you sang,' she said. 'I was proud of you.'

Ms Rose went off into the night, arm in arm with her friend, Ms Brown.

Hayley and Maybe ran outside to gulp some fresh night air. 'Do you like really small things?' Hayley asked. 'Like ladybirds and beads and tiny stones?'

'Yes,' Maybe said. Maybe didn't say 'Maybe' any more.

'So do I!' Hayley shrieked. 'Do you like dogs?'

'Yes,' Maybe said. 'So do I!' Hayley shrieked. 'Do you like noodles?'

'Yes!' Maybe shouted.

They went on like this for ages under the wide night sky, comparing their likes and dislikes.

'This is amazing,' Maybe said.

'It isn't coincidence,' Hayley said.

'Do you get the feeling this was meant?' Maybe asked, wide-eyed.

'Yes!' Hayley screamed. 'It *is* meant!'

The big harvest moon looked down on them, a witness. The moon knew everything. The moon knew the people the people had been before; the moon

knew every single life; the moon knew the name of
all the stars.